# THE SECRET GLASS

# THE
# SECRET
# GLASS

## BERYL BAINBRIDGE

GEORGE BRAZILLER        NEW YORK

Published in the United States in 1974 by George Braziller, Inc.
Copyright © 1973 by Beryl Bainbridge
Originally published in England as *The Dressmaker* by Gerald
Duckworth & Co., Ltd.

Standard Book Number: 0-8076-0746-0
Library of Congress Catalog Number: 73-93608
Printed in the United States of America
Second Printing

To Jo, Aaron and Rudi

# THE SECRET GLASS

O

---

A FTERWARDS she went through into the little front room,
the tape measure still dangling about her neck, and allowed
herself a glass of port. And in the dark she wiped at the
surface of the polished sideboard with the edge of her flowered
pinny in case the bottle had left a ring. She could hear Marge
at the sink in the scullery, washing her hands. That tin bowl
made a deafening noise. She nearly shouted for her to stop it,
but instead she sat down on mother's old sofa, re-upholstered
in L.M.S. material bought at a sale, and immediately, in spite
of the desperate cold of the unused room, the Christmas drink
went to her head. She had to bite on her lip to keep from
smiling. The light from the hallway shone on the carpet, red
and brown and good as new from all the years she had spent
caring for it. Here at least everything was ordered, secure. The
removal of the rosewood table had been a terrible mistake,
but it was foolish to blame herself for what had happened.
There was nothing mother could take umbrage at in the whole
room – not even the little mirror bordered in green velvet with
the red roses painted on the glass – because the crack across
one corner, as she could prove, was war damage, not neglect
or carelessness. The blast from a bomb dropped in Priory
Road had knocked it off the wall, killing twelve people, in-
cluding Mrs Eccles's fancy man at the corner shop, and
cracked mother's mirror.

'Are you alright then, Nellie?'

Margo was in the doorway watching her. Mother had

7

always warned her to keep an eye on Marge. Such a foolish girl. The way she had carried on about Mr Aveyard. He hadn't been a well man, nor young, and she would have lost her widow's pension into the bargain. Fancy throwing away her independence just for the honour of siding his table and darning his combs. It had taken a lot to persuade her, but in the end she'd seen the sense in it – sent Mr Aveyard packing into the bright blue yonder; but her face, the look in her eyes for all to see – there was something indecent in the explicitness of her expression.

She'd said: 'You would only have been a drudge for him, Marge.' And Marge said: 'Yes, I know, Nellie.' But her eyes, then as now, burned with the secrets of experience.

'Let me be,' said Nellie. 'I'll be through in a moment.'

Valerie had been right about a belt for the engagement dress. It would add the final touch. She let her eyes close and dozed as if she were sitting in the sun, her two stout legs thrust out across Mother's carpet, threads of green cotton clinging to her stockings.

She was awakened by voices coming from the kitchen. She listened for a moment before getting to her feet. Rita had come in and was weeping again. She was at the age for it, but it was trying for all concerned.

'Oh, Auntie, I wish I was dead.' She didn't mean it of course.

Marge was saying, 'Shh, shh,' trying to keep her quiet.

Beyond the lace curtains something glittered. Jack had pasted strips of asbestos to protect the glass, sticky to the touch, but she could just make out a square of red brick wall and the little dusty clump of privet stuck in the patch of dirt beneath the window, all pale and gleaming like a bush in flower, frozen in moonlight. She smoothed the folds of the lace curtains, re-arranging the milky fragments of privet, distracted by the sounds from the next room. If that girl didn't stop her wingeing, the neighbours would be banging on the wall, God knows, there'd been enough disturbance for one night.

8

She went into the hall, hiding the wine glass in the pocket of her apron. She swept broken glass into a heap and wrapped the pieces in newspaper; knelt to pick out between finger and thumb fragments embedded in the dust mat at the front door. She found an imitation pearl that Marge had overlooked, lying like a peppermint on the stair. She went into the kitchen with her parcel and laid it on the table.

'Valerie Mander says her Chuck hasn't seen him in over a week,' wailed Rita.

'Ssh,' Margo said again, putting her arms about the girl to calm her, looking up at Nellie with entreaty in her eyes, no colour at all in her thin cheeks.

'That's enough, Rita. It's no use crying over spilt milk,' said Nellie. ' You're better off without him.' Which was the truth, surely, though she had not meant to shout so loud.

'Turn that gas off, Marge,' she ordered and not waiting went into the scullery to turn off the ring under the kettle.

'But we always have a cup of tea before bed,' said Rita, lifting an exhausted face in protest, and Margo said for the umpteenth time, 'Sssh, ssshh,' in that daft way.

The girl washed in the scullery while the two women prepared for bed. The reflection of her bony face, pale with loss, flittered across the surface of the tarnished mirror above the sink. She bent her head and moaned, quite worn out by the depths of her emotion. A shadow leapt against the pane of glass high on the wall among the frying pans. She looked up startled, a piece of frayed towel held to her mouth, and opened the back door to let the cat in.

She called : 'Come on Nigger, come on Nigger!'

'Shut that door!' Her aunt's voice was harsh with irritation.

'Can't the cat come in then, Auntie?'

'No, leave it out.' But Nigger was in, streaking across the lino into the kitchen, up in one bound on to the sofa, eyes gleaming.

Rita went into the hall to put away her shoes in the space

under the stairs. When she came back, Auntie Marge was standing on the table, reaching up to the gasolier with its pink fluted shades, showing a portion of leg where her nightie rode up. Nellie held her firmly by the ankle, in case she should turn dizzy.

'Where's the other half of the curtain under the stairs, Auntie Nellie?' asked Rita.

Nellie had her hair net on and her teeth out. When the gas died, her face looked bruised in the firelight. She didn't answer. She tugged at Marge's gown and told her to come down, which she did, teetering wildly for a moment on the edge of the chair before reaching the floor and going at once to the sideboard. She fiddled about among the knives and forks, bringing out a packet of American cigarettes. At the sight of them the girl's face crumpled. She flung herself on her knees and buried her head in her aunt's lap as she sat down by the fire.

'Oh Auntie,' she cried, muffled in flannel, 'I do love him.'

Nellie could see Marge's hand with the thin band of gold encircling her finger, stroking the girl's bent head. The packet of cigarettes slithered to the rug. With a puritanical flick of her wrist, Nellie flung them clear to the back of the grate.

'You daft beggar, it was a full packet.'

Margo was outraged, looking up with hatred at her sister. But she quailed before the fury of the older woman.

'Shhh,' she said over and over to the girl at her knee, gazing sullenly at the cigarettes consumed by flame.

Nellie took the newspaper parcel into the scullery. She returned and stood at the mantelpiece holding her clenched fist out over the fire. The eyes of the cat flicked wide. The flames spat. Wax melted over the coals.

Rita said, startled: 'What's that?'

'Someone knocked over the little wax man in the hall. It's broken.'

The girl sat upright, the tear-stained oblong of her face full of accusation.

'The little wax man?'

'Don't look like that, Miss. It couldn't be helped.'

Nellie sucked the pad of her finger where a splinter of glass had penetrated, adding, so that the girl would know where to apportion blame : 'Your Dad knocked it over.'

'Uncle Jack? Has Uncle Jack been, then?'

She looked from one aunt to the other, but there was no reply. Nellie bolted the back door and brought a jug of water to pour on the coals. The smoke billowed outwards. The cat sprang from its place on the sofa and went with disgust to lie on the heap of newspapers behind the door.

Auntie Margo said : 'Poor old Nigger, he doesn't like that,' beginning to laugh deep in her throat and bringing her hand up to her mouth to smother the sound. Turning her face to the grate, she stared into the dampened fire.

Rita was puzzled about Uncle Jack coming. He only came round on a Saturday with the Sunday joint.

'Did Uncle Jack come about the engagement party, then?' she wanted to know. 'Is he getting Valerie Mander a cut of meat?'

'Bed,' said Nellie, but not unkindly. By now Jack would be on the dock road, heading towards Bootle. She waited in the hallway while Rita and Marge went upstairs. She let them get settled before leaning over the stair rail to extinguish the gas light.

'Are you in?' she called after a moment.

Rita could hear the banister creaking as Nellie hauled herself up the stairs. On the dark landing her bare feet smacked against the lino.

'Are you cold, Rita?'

'Yes, auntie.'

'You best come in with us.'

She didn't want the girl having that nightmare. She hadn't had it for several weeks, but she was obviously upset, fretting herself. It was best to have her near. They'd all catch their death of cold shenanniging about in the middle of the night.

Rita climbed on to the bed and slid down between the two women, putting her head under the starched sheets to shut out the cruel night air and the heart-beat of the alarm clock set for six, thinking it absurd that she should even attempt to close her eyes when her mind wandered so restlessly back and forth in search of the happiness she had lost, and falling asleep even while her head nuzzled more comfortably into the stiff linen cover of the bolster. From time to time she whimpered; and Margo snored, curled up against Rita, with one arm flung out across the green silk counterpane, cold as glass, joir.ed to the girl by a strand of hair caught on her dry upper lip.

Nellie dreamed she was following mother down a country garden, severing with sharp scissors the heads of roses.

# 1

I T WAS late August when Valerie Mander asked Rita to
the party.

'Well, it's more of a sing-song, really,' she amended. 'But
you'll enjoy yourself. Tell your Uncle Jack you're a big girl
now.' And off she went up the street, swinging her hand-bag
and tilting her head slightly to catch the warmth of the
sun.

Rita had first seen her on the tram coming home from
work, but she hadn't let on. She had been travelling since the
Pier Head, wedged hard against the window near the plat-
form. When the tram stopped opposite the bomb site that had
been Blackler's store, she hadn't noticed the people boarding,
only moved her feet to avoid being trampled, gazing out at the
rumpled meadow on the corner of the city street; thinking
of Nellie working there at the beginning of the war, on the
material counter facing millinery, shearing with her sharp steel
scissors through the yards of silk and satin and velveteen,
taking such pride in the great bales of cloth, smoothing them
with her hands, plucking with disapproval at the minute
frayed ends. To no avail. When the roof split open, the prams
and bedding spilled from the top floor to the next, mingling
with Auntie Nellie's rolls of dress material, snaking out wan-
tonly into the burning night, flying outwards higgledy piggledy,
with the smart hats hurled from their stands, the frail gauze
veils spotted with sequins shrivelling like cobwebs, tumbling
down through the air to be buried under the bricks and the

iron girders – covered now by the grass and the great clumps of weed that sprouted flowers, rusty red and purple, their heads swinging like fox-gloves as the tram lurched round the corner and began the steep ascent to Everton Brow. Only then did she glance up and see Valerie standing with one white-gloved hand raised to clutch the leather strap for support, her head swathed in a cream turban and a diamante button clipped to the hidden lobe of her ear.

Rita hung her head to avoid involvement, hoping that Valerie would not look in her direction, ready to spring to her feet and be off when her stop came. But outside the Cabbage Hall cinema, a horse pulling its coal cart took fright at an army lorry passing too close. Feet sliding on the cobblestones, it shied sideways into the traffic. Rita hesitated, was too afraid to run in front of its hooves and heard Valerie calling her name. She was forced to walk the length of Priory Road with her, dreadfully inadequate and cheeks pink with resentment. It wasn't that she felt herself to be inferior, it was more that the overwhelming ripeness and confidence of the older girl caused her acute embarrassment. Valerie was larger than life, prancing along the pavement with her heavy body clothed in a green and white frock made by Auntie Nellie, arching her plucked brows, fluttering her eyelashes shiny with vaseline, opening and closing her moist mouth, the colour of plums. It was the glossiness of her.

'Your Auntie Nellie said you were working in Dale Street now.'

'Yes, since April.'

'What's it like, then? Alright is it, Rita?'

'Yes, it's very nice, thank you.'

'What do you do, then?' Persistent. Trying to communicate. Trotting in her wedge-heeled shoes past the red-brick houses and the small shops and the ragged plane trees, windswept on every corner.

'Not much, really. I run messages for Mr Betts sometimes.'

14

'Well, that's not much, is it?' A kind of criticism in her voice. 'I thought you were good at English?'

'Me Auntie Margo was getting me a job with her in the factory at Speke.'

'Oh yes.'

In sight now, the tin hoarding high on the wall at the corner of Bingley Road, advertising Gold Flake.

'Auntie Nellie said they weren't a nice class of girl.'

They walked under the lettering, bright yellow and two-foot high, set against a sea of deepest blue, one corner eaten by rust. It was Valerie that had told Aunt Nellie that she was too pale to wear bright colours . . . 'Your Rita hasn't the complexion for it' . . . and Nellie took notice of her. Until then she had felt like a pillar-box every winter, decked out in a scarlet coat with a hat and handbag to match.

They crossed the road and went into the shadow of the air-raid shelter in the middle of the street, its concrete roof blotched by rain and a black and white cat prowling its length.

It was then Valerie asked her what she did on a Saturday night, though she knew, she must have done. She knew what Valerie did. Mrs Mander told Nellie all about her daughter's opportunities and what young man was courting her and how she'd been to a tea-dance at Reece's Ballroom and an evening do at the Locarno and what the fellow at the Ladies' Hot Pot Supper night had said about her. Nellie discussed it often with Margo, and neither of them seemed to think it strange that what was alright for Valerie was all wrong for other girls living in the street. Just fast, they were. But then Valerie, as Auntie Nellie never tired of reiterating, was a lovely girl and she did know how to take care of herself.

\*     \*     \*

Aunt Nellie had just sent the man from the Pru on his way, richer by her sixpence a week, when Rita got home. It was

15

for her funeral, so that Jack wouldn't have the expense. Around her neck she wore her tape measure like a scarf and a row of pins stuck in the bodice of her black dress. On Sundays she exchanged the white measure for a fox fur, holding the thin little paws in her hand as she went on her own to the church. She stood at her pastry board in the scullery, coating three pieces of fish with flour. She told Rita to set the table, adding: 'Get a move on, chuck. I've Mrs Lyons coming for a fitting after tea.'

'I met Valerie Mander on the tram,' said Rita, collecting plates from the shelf above the cooker. 'They're having a party on Saturday.'

She took the plates into the kitchen and left them on the sideboard, while she removed the table runner and the yellow vase full of dressmaking pins.

'I know,' Nellie said. 'Well, it's more of a sing-song, really. What was she wearing?'

'She asked me.'

Rita unfolded the white cloth and smoothed it flat on the table. Aunt Nellie was so surprised she came through from the scullery with the frying pan in her hand.

'What did you say to her?'

'I said thank you very much.'

'Oh dear, I don't know that it's wise. I'm not at all sure.'

She shook her head and went to put the pan back on the stove. Rita arranged the plates, the knives and forks, the china salt cellar, a memento from Blackpool, the water jug, the pudding spoons and the three Woolworth glasses. Still Nellie kept silent. Only the fat hissing in the pan as the fish cooked. Rita sat on a chair sideways to the table, fingering the edge of the cloth embroidered with daisies, staring at the wall with her pale eyes patient. There was a picture of a landscape above the sewing machine: a blue lake and a swan sitting on the water and the green grass fading into a cloudy sky. There was also the window framed in blackout curtains showing a brick wall and a wooden door that opened on to the alleyway,

16

through which Auntie Margo would come presently to persuade Nellie. She watched Nigger the cat crawl silently along
the wall of the roof of the out-house where her aunt kept the
dolly tub and the mangle.

Nellie called : 'What about your Uncle Jack coming?'

'Valerie Mander said to tell him I was a big girl now.'

She looked at her aunt and saw she was smiling. She was
all admiration for the lovely girl, so outspoken. She nodded
her head wonderingly, jiggling the frying pan about to stop
the fish from sticking. 'That Valerie,' she observed, 'she's a
card.'

*    *    *

As soon as Margo came in, the food was put on the table.
She sat at the edge of the hearth like a man, splaying her
knees wide and rolling a cigarette.

'Sit decent,' said Auntie Nellie, scraping margarine from a
dish and covering her bread sparingly.

It was one of Marge's irritating habits to ignore what was
on her plate till it had gone like ice and then she would say,
'By heck, Nellie, this is blooming cold.' Some nights she was
quite dry about her day at the factory, telling them in accurate
detail the remarks screamed by her fellow-workers above the
noise of the machines. She said she couldn't repeat everything
they said because she had to be guarded as careless talk cost
lives. Nellie got all exasperated and said that was foolishness,
it was more like some of those women needed their mouths
washing out with carbolic soap. Marge said that ten minutes
before the whistle blew for the end of the day shift, the dis-
abled left by the side gate, two hundred of them, in chairs,
on crutches, limping and lurching down the invalid ramp on
to the pavement – like a hospital evacuating at the start of a
fire. Shortly afterwards came the speed merchants on bicycles,
streams of them, ringing the little bells on their handlebars,
wheeling in formation out of the main gates and swooping

17

away down the hill to the town. How rough they were, how quick to take offence and come to blows. The women were worse than the men. Mr Newall, the foreman of her section, was given the glad eye by a different girl each week. But tonight Margo had nothing to tell them. She sat gloomily at the side of the empty grate, rubbing the tips of her fingers through her sparse sand-coloured hair, jerking her neck from side to side as if she were keeping time to some tune in her head. She listened to the six o'clock news before joining them at the table. She stirred her tea so savagely that some spilled into the saucer.

'What's up with you, then?' asked Nellie aggressively, as if it were a personal affront to her that Marge was out of sorts.

'It's the machines, they get on my nerves. Everyone complains of their nerves.'

'Well, it's your own fault,' Nellie said with satisfaction. 'You had no need to go into munitions in the first place.'

'Get away. I was requisitioned.'

'That job at Belmont Road Hospital was quite good enough.'

They stared at each other with hostility, their mouths munching food.

Rita said: 'Was that where those naughty girls were?' They both turned and looked at her, sitting in her pink frock with the white cotton collar that could be removed and washed separately. 'The girls with the shaved heads – to stop them running away?'

She had a picture in her head of a green tiled hall and a long corridor with its floor shining with beeswax and two figures walking towards her in dressing-gowns and slippers. Above the thin stalks of their necks two naked heads with lidless eyes and sunken mouths and on each fragile curve of skull nothing but a faint down that quivered as they moved. Like birds fallen from a nest.

'Who told her that?' Margo demanded, though she knew.

18

Nellie held her to one side as if she were listening to the wireless.

'Who told her a daft thing like that?' persisted Marge.

'Auntie Nellie said they had things in their hair.' She wished she had not spoken.

'You don't go to hospital for nits, Rita.'

Auntie Nellie stiffened in disgust.

'You're so common, Marge. That factory has coarsened you beyond belief.'

A shred of potato dropped from her lips to the plate. Mortified, she dabbed at her chin with a serviette, shaking her head sorrowfully.

'You're a foolish girl. I thank God, mother has been spared from seeing the way you've turned out.'

It was as if she were talking about a cake that hadn't risen properly. Rita could tell Auntie Margo was giddy with indignation. It wasn't a tactful remark to make to someone who had spent ten hours on the factory floor, clad in cumbersome protective clothing, grease daubed on her face and a white cloth bound about her head. It was alright for Auntie Nellie to live grimly through each day, doing the washing, trying to find enough nourishment to give them, sewing her dresses – she was only marking time for the singing to come in the next world and her reunion with Mother. It was different for Margo, a foolish girl of fifty years of age; she needed to come home, now, and find that somebody waited. How colourless were her lips, how dark the shadows beneath her eyes.

'Rita,' cried her aunt, looking at her across the table severely, 'those naughty girls, as your Auntie Nellie saw fit to call them, had a flipping sight more wrong with them than nits. It wasn't only their heads they shaved neither.'

And she broke into a cackle of laughter, eyes growing moist, leaning back in her chair at the joke. She was silent then, having gone as far as she dared, contenting herself with a mocking grin worn for the benefit of Nellie, tears of amusement at the corners of her glittering eyes.

19

When the meal was finished Nellie said : 'Rita, tell your Auntie Marge about Valerie Mander.'

She spoke coldly, on her dignity, making a great show of siding the table before taking the dishes to the sink. Margo half-rose to help, because Nellie, when put out, could appear to be suffering, her white hair plastered to her head in waves and a kirby grip to keep it neat, and that disappointed droop to her mouth. But she sat down again at this.

'What about Valerie Mander?'

'She asked me to a party.'

'She never,' said her aunt, looking at her in astonishment.

'She did. On Saturday.'

'What does your Auntie Nellie say?'

'She doesn't know if it's wise.'

They both looked down at the surface of the white table-cloth, thinking it over. On the beige wall the eight-day clock chimed the half-hour. In the kitchen they could hear Nellie swishing her hands about in the water to make it seem she was above listening.

'Do you want to go, then?'

'I don't know.'

'Won't you be shy?'

'I'm not shy.'

She met her aunt's eye briefly, and away again, looking at the dull black sewing machine with its iron treadle still tilted from the pressure of the dressmaker's foot.

'She's not got anything to wear,' Nellie said, coming to stand in the doorway, twisting her hands about in her apron to dry them.

'If that doesn't beat the band! You put dresses on the backs of half the women in the street and you say our Rita's got nothing to wear.'

Nellie had to see the fairness of that. She was never un-reasonable. She supposed she could alter something in time if the child was really keen. Neither of them looked at Rita to see what she felt. Or they could pool their clothing coupons and go to George Henry Lees' for a new frock. That might be best.

They were interrupted by the arrival of Mrs Lyons, come for her fitting. Rita curled herself up on the sofa with a library book and the cat. She murmured 'Good-evening' to Mrs Lyons, keeping her eyes down to the printed page as the stout lady stepped out of her skirt and stood in her slip on the rug.

Nellie put a match to the fire so that Mrs Lyons wouldn't catch her death. She grudged every morsel of coal burned in summer time, but she couldn't afford to lose her customers. Even so, the room took some time to warm, and it wasn't till Mrs Lyons had left that the benefit could be felt. Nellie made a pot of tea before getting ready for bed, spooning the sugar into Marge's cup and hiding the basin before Marge could help herself. The aunts put on their flannel nightgowns over their clothes and then undressed, poking up the fire to make a blaze before removing their corsets. The girl sat withdrawn on the sofa, stroking the spine of the cat, while the two women grunted and twisted on the hearth rug, struggling to undo the numerous hooks that confined them, until, panting and triumphant, they tore free the great pink garments and dropped them to the floor, where they lay like cricket pads, still holding the shape of their owners, and the little dangling suspenders sparkling in the firelight. Dull then after such exertions, mesmerised by the heat of the fire, the aunts stood rubbing the flannel nightgowns to and fro across their stomachs, breathing slow and deep. After a while they sat down on either side of the fender and removed their stockings. Out on the woollen rug, lastly, came their strange yellow feet, the toes curled inwards against the warmth.

'Rita,' said Nellie, picking up the half-furled corsets, rolling them tidily like schoolroom maps, 'what sort of dress shall it be for the party?'

'It's not a party,' said Rita. 'It's just a bit of a sing-song.'

She said she didn't know what the fuss was about. She

didn't want anything altered nor did she need a new frock. She knew she would have to go, if only for the sake of Margo. Left to herself, she mightn't have bothered. But at some point on Saturday Margo would start to apply rouge and powder, saying she was thinking of popping along to the Manders to keep the child company. And Nellie would say she was pushing herself, and they would start to argue, until turning to her they would remind each other of the time, telling her she must hurry, comb her hair, change her frock.

'Don't you want to look nice?' cried Nellie.

But Rita wouldn't discuss it any further. She went upstairs on her own to bed, leaving them muttering by the fire.

# 2

---

J ACK came promptly at four-thirty. He parked his van in the back alley and carried the Sunday joint wrapped in newspaper. He wore his Homburg hat and his overcoat.

'Have you got a cold, then?' asked Nellie, for it was a warm afternoon and the sun was shining somewhere beyond the dark little houses.

He had brought a piece of pork and some dripping and he put them on a plate high on the shelf so that the cat would leave it alone.

'Where's Rita?' he asked, removing his coat and going into the hall to hang it over the banisters.

At the foot of the stairs he cracked his ankle bone against the little iron stand set in the floor.

'That blooming thing,' he said, hobbling into the kitchen. 'God knows why they put the damn thing where you can trip over it.'

'What thing?' said Nellie, not understanding him.

'That umbrella stand. One of these days I'll break me blooming neck.'

'I never trip over it,' she said.

He lay down on the sofa with his feet on a newspaper and his hat still on his head. He always lay down when he came to Nellie's; she was forever telling him to rest and he mostly felt tired as soon as he set eyes on her. He didn't say much when Nellie told him Rita had gone with Marge to have her hair set for a party. But then it wasn't his province any more.

When his wife had died leaving him with Rita not five years old he had suggested that Nellie pack up the house in Bingley Road and come to live with him in Allerton. But she wouldn't. She said Mother would never have approved and where would she put the furniture? She was right of course – she was too old to be uprooted. Nellie knew about death – she was his right hand man, so to speak. Three sisters in infancy; Sally with the consumption, though Marge insisted it was a broken heart; Mother, Uncle Wilf, and George Bickerton, Marge's husband, dying with influenza within six months of returning from France. The last four had passed away in the little back bedroom upstairs. It was not as if Nellie cared to leave a house that held so many memories of departure. Grieved as she had been to say good-bye to mother, it was only in the nature of a temporary farewell. She had merely sent Mother ahead on a journey and would catch up with her later. It would never do to leave her post till her call came. So he sold his own home and moved with Rita into the two rooms above his butcher's shop in Anfield. Nellie was a wonderful woman. She came every morning and did for them and took the child out for an airing and put her to bed at night. But several times she took her back to Bingley Road, because she couldn't neglect the dressmaking, and it didn't seem sensible to troop out after tea, in winter, on the tram, all that way. It became a regular thing. After a time the child copied her aunts and called him Uncle Jack. He tried sleeping in the little boxroom at weekends to see more of her, but it wasn't convenient. And Nellie looked after her beautifully, making her little dresses, and always seeing she had clean white socks, and putting her hair in rags every night to make it curl. And later Nellie was very strict about her education and her homework – only the bombing was at its worst and the child was in the shelters at night, and then the school she attended had a direct hit and a lot of her friends were evacuated. Marge used to say it was all wrong for the child to live with them, they were too old, they hadn't the patience. But that was nonsense. Nellie had

24

never raised her voice to the girl, never said a bad thing to her. Marge had gone on about the nightmare Rita had from time to time. She said it wasn't natural for a young girl to have such nasty dreams, at least not the same one every time. Nellie said it was growing pains. Dr Bogle said the same. Nellie was livid with Marge for taking the child to the doctor behind her back. Most of the time he too forgot that Rita was not Nellie's daughter, but his. And she did favour the aunts in appearance. She was in their mould – nothing of his dead wife that he could see : like Marge in feature, with a mouth so pale that the upper lip seemed outlined in brown pencil, making it prominent, and with Marge's slightly frantic eyes, startled, owing to the width between brow and lid. But she was Nellie's creation. It was as if the dressmaker had cut out a pattern and pinned it exactly, placing it under the sewing machine and sewing it straight as a die, over and over, so that there was no chance of a gap in the seams.

Even more like Nellie, he thought, when Rita came in with Marge, face flushed red from the dryer and her hair stuck dry as a bone to her small head.

'My word,' he said, 'we do look a bobby dazzler !' though secretly he wondered what had happened to her nice brown hair – so little of it left and that all curled up.

'Have you had it cut then?' he asked. But she had gone out into the back yard to look for the cat. 'How much did it cost?' he wanted to know, half sitting up and putting his hand in his pocket.

'Never you mind,' said Margo, 'it's my treat.'

There was something restless about her, agitated. She strode about the room picking things up and putting them down, forgetting about the cigarette she held between her fingers. She was forever going into the scullery to bend down and re-light it at the gas jet under the kettle.

'You'll not have a hair left on your head one of these days,' warned Nellie, putting the Saturday tea on the table.

He ate his tea lying down. Nellie propped his head up

25

with pillows and balanced his plate on his chest. They had a tin of salmon that a customer had given him in return for a favour. He couldn't tell Nellie how he got it because she didn't approve of the black market. Instead he said he'd had it in the cupboard since the beginning of the war. They listened to Toy Town on the wireless and Marge stood at the mantelpiece, covering her mouth with her hand, her eyes all screwed up as if she were in pain, pretending it was Ernest the policeman she found comic, though he knew it was him.

'What's so funny, Marge?' he demanded, offended.

And she said : '*Rigor mortis* will set in if you stay like that much longer.'

He had to smile at that even though Nellie was tut-tutting. He struggled to sit upright on the sofa and put his dish down on the table. Marge had always had a sense of humour – dry, bitter at times – but she was good company. Sometimes it was as if Nellie was a damn sight too worthy for this world, making him feel he was perpetually in church, or remembering mother who had died when he was seven, all lowered voices and pious talk. He looked at Rita, but she was stolidly eating – not a trace of a smile, the colour quite faded from her cheeks.

At seven Marge went upstairs and came down in a peach crêpe dress with a necklace round her neck that had belonged to his wife. He'd offered it to Nellie, but she said she had no need of such fripperies, and it was hardly suitable for Rita.

'What's all this, then?' asked Nellie, and Marge said she was just popping round to the Manders' with Rita, to keep an eye on her.

'You weren't asked,' said Nellie.

'Get away,' Margo said, and proceeded to put powder on her cheeks.

He could tell Nellie was put out about something.

'Do you want to go?' he asked. 'Don't worry about me. I'll put me feet up and listen to Saturday Night Theatre.'

At this she made a funny little gesture of contempt with her

26

elbows, flapping them like a hen rising from its perch in alarm.

'Not me,' she said.

So he lay down again and placed the Saturday Echo over his eyes to be out of it. He could hear them talking in whispers out of deference to him, trying to get Rita to hurry up and change. 'In a minute,' she kept saying, 'I'll go in a minute.' And before she went upstairs he distinctly heard her say, 'That was my mam's, wasn't it?' and he opened his eyes and she was at the fireplace staring at Marge's neck, half reaching up her hand to touch the necklace about Marge's throat. God knows how she knew that. He was quite startled, screwing up the side of the newspaper and damaging the Curly Wee cartoon with his clenched fist. But she didn't touch Marge; she peered as if she were short-sighted, leaving Marge standing there with her own hand up to the cheap link of pearls and her mouth all red and bold with lipstick.

He closed his eyes again, and soon Nellie sat down at the sewing machine and spun the wheel, pressing the treadle up and down rapidly, running material under the stabbing needle, settling into the rhythm of it, in her element. As long as he could remember, Nellie had played the machine, for that's how he thought of it. Like the great organ at the Palladium cinema before the war, rising up out of the floor and the organist with his head bowed, riddled with coloured lights, swaying on his seat in time to the opening number. Nellie sat down with just such a flourish, almost as if she expected a storm of applause to break out behind her back. And it was her instrument, the black Singer with the handpainted yellow flowers. She had been apprenticed when she was twelve to a woman who lived next door to Emmanuel Church School : hand sewing, basting, cutting cloth, learning her trade. When she was thirteen Uncle Wilf gave her a silver thimble. She wasn't like some, plying her needle for the sake of the money, though that was important : it was the security the dressmaking gave her – a feeling that she knew something, that

27

she was skilled, handling her materials with knowledge; she wasn't a flibbitygibbet like some she could mention. For all that she lifted the tailor's dummy out from its position under the stairs coquettishly, holding it in her arms like a dancing partner, circling the arm-holes with chalk, stroking the material down over the stuffed breast, standing back to admire her work with her mouth clamped full of little pins, tape measure about her neck.

When the knock came at the front door he was almost asleep. He opened his eyes in bewilderment and saw Marge on her chair by the grate, and Nellie, her foot arrested in mid-air trying to recognise the hand at the door. He rubbed his eyes and stood upright, smoothing his clothes to be respectable. They all listened. Rita opened the front door. A strange voice, like on the films, drawling. She brought him into the kitchen. He was well-fed, dressed in uniform and he had been drinking. A great healthy face, with two enquiring eyes, bright blue, and a mouth which when he spoke showed a long row of teeth, white and protruding. It was one of those Yanks. Jack was shocked. Till now he had never been that close. They were so privileged, so foreign; he had never dreamt to see one at close quarters in Nellie's kitchen, taking Rita and Marge, one on each arm and bouncing them out of the house. He ran to the door to watch them go, linking arms, heads bowed, like they were doing the Palais Glide.

'I didn't know there would be Yanks,' he said.

'There's no harm,' said Nellie. 'Valerie Mander knows how to conduct herself.'

But he was bothered. He couldn't lie down and compose himself; the sheer fleshiness of the young American disturbed him – the steak they consumed, the prime pork chops, the volume of butter and bacon. He remembered all the things he had read : the money they earned, the food they digested, the equipment they possessed. He'd seen them down by Exchange Station, pressing young girls up against the wall, mouth to mouth as if eating them, and jeeps racing up

Stanley Street full of military police and great dogs on metal chains with their jaws open and their pink gums exposed.

'I didn't know there'd be Yanks,' he said again, walking up and down the room in his green waistcoat that Nellie had made and his gun metal trousers.

'Did you notice what our Rita said about that necklace?' he asked in astonishment.

But Nellie was placing the top half of Mrs Lyons' grey costume under the steel clamp, her head bent and all her concentration on the lovely width of serge beneath her fingers.

# 3

I N THE circumstances Margo couldn't help feeling that she
was superfluous. The party was not a knees-up for the
neighbours with a few of Cyril Mander's business acquaint-
ances on show to make a bit of a splash. She didn't suppose
there would be any political talk or views on how the war was
going. Nor would there be fancy cakes and a few bottles of beer
on the sideboard. The house was swarming with American
soldiers and young women in their gladrags. The three-piece
suite was quite submerged. On the hall table there was a pile
of mustard-coloured caps, one upon the other, like a plate of
sandwiches. She was struck, as usual, by the dazzling display
of lights, in the hall, the front room, the kitchen. She stood
blinking, helped out of her duster coat by the young man
who had escorted them the few yards up the street. 'Thank
you,' she said, and repeated it for Rita, who said nothing
at all, allowing the pink cardigan to be removed from her
shoulders. Valerie was wearing a black skirt with a patent-
leather belt about her waist. She was bubbling over with
excitement and generosity, explaining that she thought Rita
would never have come if Chuck hadn't fetched her. Chuck
nodded his head lazily, and she put her arm through his and
pressed close to him.

It occurred to Margo that it was a funny name for a
grown man. Surely the whites of his eyes were a shade too
milky and the curve of his eyeball somewhat extreme. She
remembered all the stories circulated about English girls
marrying GIs and having black children. You could never be

sure until it was too late. Jack said all the decent Americans had left the country before D-Day, ready for the thrust into Europe; only the riff-raff remained – canteen staff and garage mechanics. Mrs Mander couldn't wait to tell her all about him. Valerie had met him at a dance a week ago and he'd taken her out nearly every night since, to the State Restaurant, the Bear's Paw, to the repertory company, to some hotel over on the Wirral, very posh by all accounts.

'The repertory company?' said Marge, bewildered.

'To a play,' said Mrs Mander, 'with actors.'

'He must have money to burn.'

'Well, there's no harm in that, and he does seem keen, doesn't he?'

She peered at Marge, trying to gauge what she was thinking, scrutinising her mouth as if she were deaf and needed to lip-read.

'They certainly seem very thick,' Margo said, watching the young man at the fireplace with his hand dangling over the white shoulder of Valerie Mander. On his wrist, strong black hairs and a watch of solid gold.

'Oh, they are,' cried Mrs Mander gaily, putting a glass of whisky into her hand and leaving her, waddling out of the doorway in her midnight blue dress with the enormous skirt.

Cyril Mander was playing the piano very slowly as if he weren't sure of the tune. He was in his best blue suit, showing a lot of white cuff, his silver links catching the light. On the top of the piano was a jug full of lupins and a photograph of son George in his sailor's uniform. Every time Cyril struck a chord, the flowers trembled and showered petals on the keys. None of the young couples heeded his playing. Valerie was looking through the gramophone cabinet for records.

Marge wondered whether the Manders were wise, filling the house with strangers and letting them behave any way they pleased. There was a war on, of course, and she knew attitudes were different, but there was such a thing as a

31

responsibility. It would serve Mrs Mander right if she became the proud grandmother of a bouncing piccaninny.

Sipping her drink and shuddering at its strength, she went out into the hall to look for Rita. The coats on the banisters had slid to the floor. She could see Rita's cardigan lying all crumpled. As she bent to retrieve the clothing, Cyril Mander came behind her and seized her by the hips. She was quite embarrassed. He told her she must come and meet people – she mustn't be a spoil sport. He took the coats from her, spilling them carelessly on the stairs. Clutching the cardigan, she was propelled into the living room. Jack detested him – said he was a profiteer and a swine, which was a bit unkind. Margo rather liked him, though not at such close quarters. He'd made a lot of money out of scrap metal and he did tend to be showy; but that was preferable to being moody like Jack, or martyred like Nellie.

'What do you think of our Valerie's latest acquisition?' he whispered, crumpling her shoulder in his big hand and shaking her like a doll.

The heat from the fire was unbearable. Such a reckless use of coal, and summer not yet ended.

'I like the new grate,' she said.

But he wasn't listening. There was no mantelpiece : nowhere to stand her glass. Just a thin little ledge of cream tiles, and above it a fancy mirror with scalloped edges. She could see her own face reflected – damp, as if she were rising up out of the sea, with staring eyes, and behind her head young couples dancing cheek to cheek, circling and gliding out of the mirror.

'This is my girl from up the street,' said Cyril, thrusting her forward at an angle, yet still retaining a grip on her shoulder.

'How d'you do,' Margo said to the two young men who stood on the hearthrug, shaking hands with one, who smiled at her with his beautifully rounded cheeks dimpling in welcome and went away to refill her glass, while she held Cyril upright and was ready to save him if he toppled forwards.

32

She sweated under the combined heat of Cyril and the fierce flames that roared up the chimney. She took her replenished glass when it came, endeavouring to stand a little straighter, sipping the drink rapidly before Cyril should spill it for her. She had last tasted whisky four years ago at the height of the blitz when an A.R.P. warden had given her some to steady her nerves. She remembered the occasion with bitterness, having slipped on the kerbstone in the blackout on her way home, raising a bump on her chin. Nellie said she was drunk.

'This little lady,' Cyril was saying, 'is a soldier's wife, through and through.'

Seized by an abrupt melancholy, he released Marge and stared down at the carpet.

'Where is your husband stationed, mam?' The American looked at her with his head tilted deferentially to one side.

She was convulsed, choking on her drink. How richly oiled was the hair on his head, how smooth the skin beneath his eyes. Her chest heaved with the effort of suppressing laughter.

'Up there,' she wheezed, rolling her eyes in the direction of the ceiling.

'Dear God,' said Cyril, shaking his head and yawning.

Deserting the three-piece suite, the couples rose to Ambrose and his Orchestra, clutching each other in the centre of the room. Standing on the leather settee with legs bent, as if to take an unlikely leap into the dark, Cyril struggled to open the window. Exhausted, he sank to his knees and leaned his forehead peacefully against the cushions, back turned on his jostling guests, the yellow curtains shifting gently in the draught.

'Dear me!' remarked Margo. 'Mr Mander is well away and no mistake.'

The young man with the dimples in his cheeks asked her to dance. She went with streaming eyes, fox-trotting across the carpet in his arms. Silly really, in such a tiny room – bumping into the sideboard, tripping over the rug. She was breathless before she had completed one turn of the floor.

33

'Are you alright, mam?' he asked her, mistaking the marks on her cheeks for tears of distress.

'Yes, yes,' she assured him, and turned her head away for fear she should laugh again. It was no use explaining how she felt about her dead husband from another war, it was so long ago. She hardy knew him to begin with, let alone remembered him now, so many years on. She had always felt he was more Nellie's relation than hers, seeing Nellie had nursed him toward death. Whenever she had tiptoed upstairs, Nellie had told her to go away, he was resting; and even at the funeral it was Nellie that did enough crying for both of them.

It was a relief when the record ended and the young man took his hand from her wrist. Wiping her eyes, she left him to look for her glass and refill it from the bottle on the sideboard. She didn't feel guilty; it hadn't been come by honestly, so why shouldn't she have the benefit of it? Years ago Jack had given her a pad of cottonwool soaked in whisky for the toothache. 'Get rid of them,' said Nellie contemptuously. 'You don't want any truck with those. Get yourself some nice new teeth.' And she did, though it took her six years to pay for them. Rita went to the dentist regularly – but then times had changed. Rita? She went into the hall to search for her. The door was open on to the street. Mrs Evans at No. 9 was leaning out of her bedroom window to get a shuftie at the goings on. Margo caught a glimpse of a green velvet dress and a tall soldier with his hands in his pockets lounging against the privet hedge.

She hesitated, and at that moment Mrs Mander called from the kitchen : 'Marge, Marge, give us a hand with the eats!'

She couldn't refuse, not being an invited guest in the first place.

'Our Rita's on the step,' she said, 'with a soldier. There's no harm, is there?'

'Get away,' said Mrs Mander. 'She's seventeen.'

The display of food on the table was quite pre-war in style : a whole ham lying in a bed of brown jelly, a bowl of real butter, like a slab of dripping, white as milk; on a dinner plate, piled high, a pyramid of oranges. Margo sat down on a chair and looked.

'It's Chuck,' said Mrs Mander. 'He insisted.'

'I was never in the limelight, was I?' asked Margo.

'You what?' Mrs Mander paused from slicing bread.

'You could never say I was made much of?'

'You've been drinking, Marge,' said Mrs Mander, relieved.

'I've never felt,' continued Margo, picking at the ham with her fingers, 'that people took enough notice. I have got thoughts.'

'Oh yes,' said Mrs Mander.

'You've got Cyril and George and your Valerie . . .'

'Well, you've Rita.'

'She's not easy, you know. We've got her and we haven't.'

At that moment Chuck came into the room and asked for an orange.

'We're going to play games,' he said; 'I want an orange,' taking one from the dinner plate and beginning to tear the peel from it.

'That's nice,' said Mrs Mander. 'What sort of a game?'

'Napoleon's eye,' said Chuck. 'Valerie knows it.' And he went out with the fruit clamped in his sharp wolfish teeth.

After a time there was a lot of activity in the hall. Girls sat down giggling in the kitchen alongside Margo. She held her head up and tried to concentrate. Shrieks came from the front room. A young woman in a grey costume appeared, wringing her right hand and moaning with mock terror. 'It's awful,' she cried, 'it's really awful.'

One by one the girls were taken into the other room. At last they came for Margo.

'Get off,' she protested. But they blindfolded her and led her away. She was aware of men's hands holding her, spinning her round in a circle.

'You are now on the flag ship,' drawled an unfamiliar voice, and she was lifted in the air and rocked like a baby.

'Oh, oh, oh,' she screamed, little flecks of light dancing before her eyes.

'It is a rough and stormy night. You are about to meet Napoleon, greatest of British admirals.'

Her hand was held in a dry palm. She sat down on something soft and yielding.

'How do you do! Pleased to meet you.'

'How do you do,' repeated Marge, her hand pumping up and down.

'Feel his head,' said the voice, and she stroked at something slippery, like satin – quilted like a tea cosy.

'Get away,' she screeched, 'it's a cosy.'

'This is his good arm – this is his bad arm.'

She felt a bandaged wrist, a bulky object. All around, the air was filled with whispers, instructions, smothered bursts of merriment. She was like a dog, pointing her nose to scent the wind, sitting there in her best crêpe dress, helpless.

'This is Napoleon's good eye,' said a girl's voice, and her nails flicked skin. She could feel the quivering eyeball beneath the lid.

'And this is Napoleon's bad eye –'

All at once her finger was seized firmly by the root and stabbed fiercely downward. Into moist juicy flesh. She screamed thinly, over and over, shaking with revulsion while the cloth was torn from her eyes and she saw Chuck grinning at her with the obscenely fingered orange lying in his palm. Woken by the commotion, Cyril stirred by her side. He pulled her down across him and she lay with beating heart against his white shirt.

'It's not Napoleon,' she protested, 'it's Nelson,' and closed her eyes.

When she awoke, the room was in darkness save for firelight. There was a couple in the armchair against the wall

36

and a young man dozing on the floor. She struggled upright, disentangling herself from the still-slumbering Cyril, thinking of Rita. Mrs Mander was in the kitchen amidst a debris of food.

'Feeling better, are you?' she asked. 'I saved you some ham.' And she handed her a plate lined with pink meat and a slice of bread and butter.

'I must find our Rita.'

There was a sour taste in Margo's throat and she felt as if she'd been up all night working.

'She's most like upstairs,' said Mrs Mander. 'They're playing sardines.'

'Sardines?'

'Somebody hides and whoever finds them like, hides with them. You know – girls and boys.' She winked a mascaraed eye. 'Didn't you ever play it?'

'They got the last game wrong,' said Margo crossly. 'It was never Napoleon.'

She resolutely put down her plate of ham and went into the hall. The trouble with the Manders' house was that it pretended to be different from hers and Nellie's. No landmarks anywhere. Everything old had been ripped out and replaced by something modern, unfamiliar. A recess lit by a lamp where the cupboard under the stairs would have been; a whole window of glass put in the hall at the side of the front door. To give more light, Mrs Mander said. Light was meant to be outside – that was the point of living inside. And anyway it was sheer foolishness, considering the bombing could start up again. There might even be doodlebugs, and they'd be sorry they hadn't kept the bricks.

On the bottom stair there was a couple courting.

'Excuse me,' she said. 'I want to get up there.'

They made themselves small, squeezing against the rail. The war had made everyone lax, openly immodest. It wasn't only the Yanks. There were all the jokes she heard at work about the girls in the Land Army getting in the hay with the Italian

37

prisoners of war, and Up with the Lark and To Bed with a Wren.

Upstairs the place was in darkness. She tried putting the light on in the front bedroom, but there were bodies everywhere – on the bed, on the floor – so she turned it off quick. But not before she had caught a glimpse of Valerie lying on her mother's bed, dazed in Chuck's military arms.

'Valerie,' she said loudly, 'where's our Rita?' And Valerie replied in a funny strangled voice: 'She's hiding, Auntie Marge.'

'Rita!' called Margo, thoroughly alarmed.

The back bedroom was empty. No breathing, no sounds. She put the light on. There was a small bed and a big wardrobe. She stood not knowing what to do; it was not in her nature to make a scene in someone else's house. Nellie would look under the bed and into the wardrobe, but this was Valerie's room, private, full of her belongings and her secret jars of face cream. It was a shock to find the room so plainly furnished – oil cloth on the floor and a cheap little square of carpet bought at Birkenhead market. It was not as she expected. Where was the flamboyancy, the style that showed in the clothes she wore? She opened the wardrobe and looked inside. There was Rita among the dresses and the pin-striped suits, staring out, not touching the young man with the long bony face.

After a moment of surprise Rita said: 'This is Ira. He's an American.'

'How do you do?' said Margo, and Rita stepped out of the wardrobe and he followed.

They walked ahead of her down the stairs: casually, not hurrying. In the kitchen she saw his face plainly; pale eyes, pale mouth, colourless hair. They were like brother and sister. Not at all threatening, no bulk to him, thin as a whippet, with big hands dangling and feet like an elephant. Rita was perfectly composed, sitting down at the table and sipping thoughtfully at a glass of dandelion and burdock. He said nothing,

38

leaning against the wall as if he was sleepy, looking at the girl.

'Do you want to go now, Auntie? Have you had enough?'

'Well, I think we better. I haven't brought the key . . .'

'And Auntie Nellie will be waiting up,' said Rita, finishing the sentence for her, thanking Mrs Mander very much for a lovely party, not looking at the young man, going out into the hall. Mrs Mander gave Marge a serviette full of ham for Nellie and a pickled onion – to placate her, though she didn't say so.

'Tarrah, Valerie!' called Rita up the stairs. 'Thank you very much for having me.'

It was warm in the street, dark and sheltered. From two roads away the sound of a tram.

'It's not that late, then,' said Margo wonderingly.

\*　　\*　　\*

'You look a fair sight,' said Nellie, eyeing Margo's washed out face and the lipstick smeared at the corners of her mouth.

Mrs Lyons' costume, inside out and lined with grey taffeta, shimmered on the padded torso of the dressmaking dummy.

'Did you enjoy yourself, love?' asked Jack, of Rita.

'Yes, thank you.' And she was off upstairs to bed, not even bothering to wipe her face or clean her teeth.

'What happened?' asked Nellie. 'Who was there?'

'We played games,' Margo told her.

'Games?'

'You know, party games. Hide and seek – and dancing –'

'Hide and seek?'

'Upstairs in the wardrobes.' She fidgeted on her chair, aware that she had told a part but not the whole. 'I'm tired Nellie. I'll tell you in the morning.'

'You'll tell us now,' retorted Nellie firmly. 'It seems to have been a rum do. What about the sing-song?'

'They had none of the neighbours in,' said Margo.

'Who played the piano?'

39

'We didn't have a sing-song. There were just Yanks from the camp and friends of Valerie's.'

'Did Mrs Evans do "Bless This House"?'

'I told you, none of the neighbours were asked.' She tried hard to keep the irritation out of her voice. 'Mrs Mander saved you some ham.'

She reached in her handbag and brought out the serviette parcel.

'Very nice of her, I'm sure,' said Nellie, unwrapping it. 'Jack and I had rubber egg and boiled tomatoes.'

There was something troubling Margo, something she wanted to verbalise if she could only find the words. She wanted to get it out because it put her in a good light, made her seem responsible and right-thinking. But how to phrase it? She began: 'I wonder if it's normal for Rita to be so –' and couldn't go on.

Nellie said sharply: 'To be what?'

Margo pondered. 'So – quiet.'

It wasn't right. Jack looked at her without expression.

'I mean, she doesn't let on much, on the surface, how she's feeling.'

'Get away!' said Nellie, remembering the afternoon Jack had told Marge to give up Mr Aveyard. They all remembered it, even Margo whose thoughts were confused. Jack had driven with Rita in the van to meet Marge coming out of work at Belmont Road Hospital. She was a long time, and like all men kept waiting he was in quite a paddy when she finally got into the car. Blurting it out with no finesse, telling her he and Nellie had decided she must give Mr Aveyard the push. Marge said she didn't see why she should, and he said women of her age got foolish notions; and that made her weep. And the child, leaning her elbows on the front seats, stared at both their faces: Jack white because he was thwarted, and Marge with the tears dripping down her cheeks. At the lights on Priory Road she had leapt out of her seat and run headlong down the street. Jack had followed in the van, bellowing at her out of the window: 'You daft baggage! Learn sense woman!' 'I love him,' screeched Marge, mad with rebellion. 'I won't give him up, I won't!' And an old woman wrapped in a black knitted shawl, with a baby's hand like a brooch clawing at the front of her bosom, stopped and turned to look. Jack jumped out on to the pavement and caught up with Marge, struggled with her, tried to drag her back to the car. Twisting away from him, she ran like a girl down the side street, her hair coming out from under her hat and her heels flying. Jack thought he heard a baby crying as he passed the old woman all in black, but when he climbed into the car it was Rita. When they returned to Bingley Road, Nellie was angry with him. 'You shouldn't have,' she said, 'not in front of the child, you shouldn't have,' taking the little girl in her arms and rocking her. 'I want my Auntie Margo,' wailed the child, running to the door and not tall enough to turn the latch. There was nothing for it but to sit in the best front-room with the chair turned to the window, the lace curtains hitched up, so that she could see down the street. Waiting. Twice Nellie tried to carry the girl upstairs to bed, but she woke and broke out sobbing afresh, so they sat all night on the green plush chair. Now and then Nellie dozed and the little girl slipped on her lap and held her hand up to cover her cheek from the row of pins stuck in the bodice of her aunt's dress – then the light coming in the sky, like war being declared or mother dying, dramatic, till the bow-legged man came with his long pole and snuffed out the lamps in the street.

'I just wondered. I'm not easy in my mind,' said Margo, watching Nellie picking at the ham crushed in the paper napkin, strands of silko adhering to her skirts, and Jack packing shreds of Kardomah tea into the bowl of his pipe.

'How you can smoke that stuff beats me,' said Nellie. She stood up, grasped the dressmaking dummy in her arms, as if she was tossing the caber, and staggered the few steps into the hall. Parting the brown chenille curtains under the stairs with her foot, she trundled the dummy safely into the darkness.

41

# 4

IF I AM SEEN, thought Rita, I shall deny it. I shall think of
nothing but the house with the cherry trees in the garden
and I won't hear what they say. She looked out of the window
of the bus and resisted the temptation to hide under the seat.
Her companion, wearing a little mustard cap tilted over one
eye, raised his long legs and rested them on the curved rail
before the window. She tried not to be agitated by his lack
of consideration. Auntie Nellie said only louts behaved in
public as if they were in the privacy of their homes. She did
notice he wore nice white socks.

All the way on the tram from Priory Road she didn't think
she would meet him. What if Auntie Nellie had an accident
and they phoned her at work to come home quick? She should
have stayed in her seat till they reached the mouth of the
Mersey Tunnel, but she found herself standing on the plat-
form as the tram swayed past the Empire Theatre, with a
picture of George Formby pasted to the wall; and she jumped
while the tram still moved, running on the pavement with her
handbag clutched to her chest. It surprised her. She didn't
look up, because that way it was more of a dream, walking
through the crowds hurrying in the opposite direction, with
the stone lions crouching on St. George's plateau across the
square and Johnny Walker high on the hoardings above the
Seamen's Hotel. When she was little, Uncle Jack had held her
hand, in the dark, and said, 'Look at his hat', and there he

42

was, all lit up and moving, his hat coming off his head and his legs marching, and the great bottle of whisky emptying as the coloured lights mathematically reduced. It's me, she thought, and it's not me, scurrying along in her macintosh, for it had rained without ceasing all summer.

'It's a helluva place,' said Ira, looking at the scarred streets and the cobblestones worn smooth by the great cart-horses that thundered down the hill to the coal yards behind Lime Street Station.

'The place we're going to,' said Rita, 'is quite nice really. Not like America, but it's nice.'

She felt better once the bus was on the dock road going out of town, past the sugar refinery of Tate and Lyle, and the warehouses, a smell of damp grain coming through the open window and the glimpses beyond the bomb sites of ships in the river.

'Uncle Jack,' she told him, 'says the slaves built the docks. On the wharves they've got posts with rings in where they chained them up.'

'Oh yes,' he said, 'it's a helluva place.'

Maybe she shouldn't have mentioned the slaves, he being American and used to coloured soldiers. She hadn't the knack of conversation; all her life she had been used to being spoken to without the need to respond, of looking at faces without imagining she was being observed. It came hard to her, the business of being alone with him. She sat weighted in her seat, distressed by his silence, her neck aching with the effort of not turning to stare at him. She would have feasted her eyes on him if others had been present, the pale saddle of freckles on the bridge of his nose, the almost invisible line of his blond eyebrow, which she had registered on a previous occasion.

They were leaving the town altogether now, the miles of docks that carried on into Bootle and beyond, winding inland away from the camouflaged depots and goods yards – not entirely countryside yet, but fields here and there separating

43

the groups of houses; allotments growing vegetables; washing hanging on a line strung between two leafy trees. They went over a little hump-backed bridge and there were water lilies floating.

'Oooh,' she went, as the bus accelerated and dipped down sharply.

'It's not far now,' she said, darting a glance at him, seeing his eyes closed as if he slept.

She hoped she had remembered the place rightly, had not mis⸱aken its situation : a corn field and ornamental gates guɑ ⸱ding a big estate, a small lodge house with a cherry tree growing against the wall. Uncle Jack had shown it to her when she was a child, on the way to a farmer he knew, to slaughter pigs. And again at the beginning of the war, to a picnic at the side of the corn-field. 'When the Germans come,' he said, 'which they will, mark my words, they'll smash the house down, quick as a flash.' 'How?' she asked, mouth open that such a thing could happen, looking in through the mullioned windows and seeing a potted geranium and a round stuffed hen with stippled breast and legs set wide apart. 'Tanks,' he had said darkly. 'Armoured tanks, drive straight at the gate and through, and Bob's your uncle.' And she saw it all, the bricks giving and the stairway collapsing, one wall with a picture still hanging on a nail, and the hen with its stuffing coming out lying under the cherry tree.

When they came to Ince Blundell and the roundabout planted with pink and mauve flowers, she thought they were near. The bus swung round the curve of the road, hugging the pavement, nudging the branches of a tree that brushed its leaves the length of the windows.

'Jesus,' said Ira, waking in alarm, his eyes filled with a blur of green whipping across the glass.

'You shouldn't say that,' she said, and could have bitten her tongue.

'Are we there?' he asked, yawning, and stretching his long arms above his head.

44

So eager was she not to miss the place that they left the bus a mile too soon, plodding along the main road lined with red-brick bungalows, the sun coming out, not strongly but shining all the same.

'Look,' she said 'at the gardens.'

And he looked, though she couldn't tell what he made of the neat hedges, the shrub roses, the crazy-paving spotted with small rock plants, white, blue and buttercup yellow. Isn't it pretty, she thought; it's so pretty. She remembered the back yard under soot in Bingley Road and the one lump of lupins coming up each year by the wash-house wall.

The road cut clear through the woods. They were forced to walk single-file because the path was so narrow. On the films she had seen women wandering down deserted country roads, dappled by sunshine, about to meet lovers or strangers, and they all swayed with a particular motion of the hips, as if they were bare under their clothes. She herself moved stiffly, she felt, like a nailed up box. She had wanted to wear a thin summer dress under her macintosh, but Auntie Nellie would have commented, and she hadn't known when she dressed that she had intended to meet the American. She wasn't clear in her mind whether it was fear on her part or a belief that he wouldn't be there, at the bus terminal, as they had arranged. She wished it could be hot and dazzling in the heat – walking hand in hand through the green glade and a rush of words because they were so close. At the moment they were strangers, the words waiting to be said, but soon it would be different, she was quite sure of that. She wished he could catch a fragrance from her hair or the folds of her sensible dress, that he would hold her hand as he had done so fleetingly in the wardrobe, that he would look at her searchingly; she was so anxious for the love story to begin. The gates were still there, set back from the road, the carved griffins on their stone posts beside the entrance, the lodge through the iron bars, windows encircled by ivy and a tree growing close to the wall. But when she ran to look through the gates into the

45

house she couldn't see into the room. In some way the lodge had retreated further into the trees.

'There was a stuffed hen,' she cried, 'with a yellow beak.'

'Hens,' he said, 'are cunning birds. Why, we had a hen at home that sat on a chair by the fire and never gave up. Not if you poured water over it.'

'Have you got pets at your house, then?'

'No, we have a dog and a goat and a mare, but we don't have no pets.'

She was mad for the way he said 'dawg', like he was a movie star, larger than life.

'I had a rabbit called Timoshenko. I kept my nightie in it.'

'You what?'

'It was a bag with ears, for me nightie. Auntie Nellie made it me. When I got the measles she sent it to a children's home in case it was infected.'

He shook his head, either in sympathy or because he didn't understand. He stood, scuffing his feet on the gravel, watching the cars as they drove past. After a moment he said, 'What we going to do now – now that we're here?'

'Just walk,' she said. 'We can't get in there, it's private.'

She tried to think where the corn-field grew, in which direction, beyond the woods or up the road. She didn't want to go ahead of him lonely any more, so she ran across the road and scrambled down into the ditch, climbing up on to the far bank with her shoes soaked and her stockings splashed with mud.

'It's a helluva place to go,' he said, looking at her across the ditch.

He stayed on the path, separated from her, as she tore a trail through the puddles of water and patches of bramble. She was amazed at the amount and variety of plants that grew in the woods, quite apart from the trees – the quantity of thorn bush and briar that assailed her on every side. It only made her the more determined; she wasn't put out.

'There's a corn field,' she cried, keeping up with him as he

46

sauntered along the pavement wtih his hands in his pockets. 'My dad took me when I was little for a picnic.'

He stopped quite still to look at her.

'Your dad?'

It had slipped out, it wasn't any part of them. She dragged her feet through the mud and wondered what Auntie Nellie would say about the state of her stockings. I fell off a tram, she thought, and a dog got at me. In spite of the worry, she began to laugh. It was daft to try and get away with it. She could see her aunt's eyebrows slanting upwards like a chinaman, bewildered: 'You fell off a tram?' Her eyebrows, grey like her hair, save at the tips which were tinged with brown, inscrutably raised in disbelief. 'I was pushed from behind, Auntie Nellie, and then this spaniel worried me.' Like in the English lessons at school, finding the most suitable word for the occurrence.

She gave little high-pitched gasps for breath, on her side of the ditch, treading the blackberries underfoot, her hair sliding down out of the brassy kirby grips, and he said: 'You gone crazy or something?'

'I'm thinking of me Auntie Nellie and what she'll make of the state I'm in.'

'You look fine to me.'

He had said it, he had noticed her. The journey on the bus, when he had so cruelly closed his eyes to shut her out, no longer mattered. The trees ended: ahead, splayed out under the weak sunshine, three acres of corn, uncut because of the bad weather, pale brown under a sky filled with frayed white clouds.

\*     \*     \*

Marge had asked Nellie to call at the corner shop on Breck Road for her ciggies. She was going to have a bite of tea with a girl from work and the shop would be closed by the time she came home. Nellie thought it a foolish thing to do, going off like that to someone's house after a hard day's work, but she couldn't interfere. There were times when Marge was adamant. It was a nuisance, of course, having to keep her dinner warm in the oven. She hated sewing with the smell of food in the air. It lingered, penetrated the fabric of the material; but what was one meal kept on the gas in a lifetime? She didn't seek to be restricting, but she'd always been a leader, even if it was in a purely domestic sense – arranging, decorating, budgeting – and Marge was a follower. She'd do what anyone wanted, provided it was silly enough. Her intentions were good, but she lacked tenacity. She was the big blaze that died down through lack of fuel. All that fuss about fire-watching in spite of her bronchitis, down into town every night to her post, prowling about the roof of the Cunard Building with her bucket of sand and her tin hat, keen as mustard at first, then sloping off home earlier and earlier, making excuses, absent without leave. She couldn't sustain it. When she came home one night with a bruise on her chin and her breath reeking of whisky, she realised herself that that was the end of her little jaunt into battle. The truth was, Nellie thought, stabbing her hat-pin into the back of her brown hat, it wasn't only Marge that found it hard to preserve interest. She too was beginning to retreat from the front line. She was forever peering out into the world, listening for the sound of the bugle, willing reinforcements to arrive. She had confided her worries to Mr Barnes, the minister at St Emmanuel's Church; but though he was a good enough man, he was naturally limited by his own maleness from understanding her problems. She was concerned that when she woke each morning to the alarm clock on the bedside table, her first thoughts were not thankfulness that she had been spared breath, but worry over mother's furniture. Did the damp warp it in winter, the sun expand it in summer? Had it deteriorated in the small hours of the night? There was dry rot, wet rot, woodworm. She lived in dread that she would be taken ill and begin to die. Marge wouldn't bother to wipe

48

with vinegar the sideboard, or draw the blinds against the warmth of a summer afternoon to ensure the carpet wouldn't fade. She was indolent. She had sewn Rita into her vest when the child was small and the winter particularly bitter. She could confide to Mr Barnes her weariness of spirit over the endless making-do with the rations, the queueing at the shops; but to admit her slavery to mahogany and rosewood was difficult, when he continually admonished her from the pulpit to consider the lilies of the field. Had they been her very own lilies she would have spent a lifetime ensuring that they too retained their glory. Brooding, she walked the length of the road, smiling briefly at one or two neighbours who nodded in her direction, clutching her shopping bag to the breast of her black tailored coat. The thought of mother's things in a sale-room, or worse in the junk shop on Breck Road, caused her pain in the region of her heart. She hoped she wasn't about to suffer a decline. She would wake at night with Marge lying beside her and remember quite vividly episodes of the past, unconnected: an outing as a child to the birthplace of Emily Brontë; Father in his broadcloth suit; Mother faded, sepia-coloured against the sky, sitting in the sparse grass on the moors, squinting into sunshine. Or she was at a desk at school with her mouth open watching a fly caught in a spiral of light, beating its wings against the panes of glass. She lay moistening her dry lips with her tongue, staring out into the dark little bedroom.

She had walked the length of Priory Road and turned at the Cabbage Hall into Breck Road and not known it, not recorded one tree or shop or item of traffic. Of course it had changed. There were bomb craters and rubble and old land-marks cleared away, but still it bewildered her that she had come so far in her mind and not been conscious of the route. Inside the corner shop she asked for Marge's ciggies.

'Good afternoon. Lovely day, isn't it?'

The woman said it was a grand day but she only kept cigarettes for her regular customers. She wore a pink turban

49

with some wax grapes pinned to left of centre, and drop ear-
rings with purple clusters. Nellie's eyes rounded in wonder.
She put her fingers on the counter and explained that Marge
was regular, always bought her ciggies here, but she was
going to be late home and she'd come instead, 'to fetch them
for her.'

'I'm sorry love, I don't know you from Laurel and
Hardy.'

'She comes every night. She's thin and she's got a green
coat and . . .'

But Nellie couldn't really say what Marge looked like,
couldn't for the life of her describe her features. After all those
years. Her eyes travelled the rows of glass jars half-filled with
sweets, such pretty colours, on shelves rising clear to the
ceiling, among advertisements for tobacco, for chocolates, a
naval man with sea spray on his cheeks, a dandy in an opera
cloak smiling down at her with eyes like Rudolf Valentino.
She stood in a circle of light, dazed by the flecks of white at
the centre of his eyes and the dust-filled rays of the sun that
shone through the topmost window of the shop.

'She always has ten Abdullah. Every night.'

'Sorry, luv. I told you.'

Nellie was deafened by her own heartbeats. She clutched
the counter for support, unable to move. There was a jar of
liquorice laces on the counter, coiled like snakes. Nellie wanted
to pick up the jar and smash it in the woman's face – there,
where the edge of her dusty hair caught fire in the sun and
the little grapes dangled.

'I'm sorry, luv, but you see how I'm placed.'

Nellie saw her placed – painted like Carmen Miranda
on a pantomime backcloth that bulged outwards and wavered
as if a gust of wind swept the shop. Faint with anger, Nellie
went out of the door and started for home. It was the third
time in one month that she had made herself ill with ungovern-
able rage over a trivial incident.

*       *       *

They were sitting at the edge of the cornfield. Apart. He hadn't held her hand or tried to kiss her. He squatted on his haunches above the ground damp from the rain and the narrow ditch that ran beside the field. She had asked him about books, and he said he didn't read much, and when she mentioned poetry he had looked at her curiously, not commenting.

'My Auntie Margo is a great reader.'

'Is that so?'

'She reads all sorts. I found a book once. She hid it in a drawer.'

'She did?'

'It was awful. You know, it was rude.'

'What kind of rude?' he asked, his eyes not quite so sleepy.

'You know, men and women.' She wished she hadn't told him.

'How come you know it was that kind of a book?'

'Don't be daft. You only had to read the first page. You must have seen books like that, you being in the army.'

'I don't have no call to read them kind of books,' he said. 'I seen pictures in magazines, but I ain't read none of them books.'

She felt he was criticising her, blaming her alongside Auntie Margo.

'I only read a bit of it,' she said defensively. 'I don't know where she got it from.'

'She didn't look to me like a woman who would read them sort of books.'

'Oh, she's deep, is Auntie Margo. She was married once to a soldier, but he died from the gas in France.'

He swung his hands between his knees and gazed out across the flat countryside, following the ribbon of highway that wound like a river into the distance.

'She was courting once when I was small, but she gave him up.'

'Courting?'

51

'She didn't care enough, she didn't fight for him.'

He wasn't comfortable with her, she could tell. Every time she looked at him it hurt that she couldn't finger his hair or touch his cheek. She wished he would put down the stick that he dug into the yellow earth, poking the soil, not paying her attention.

'Let's go,' she said. 'The sea's over there.'

'If you like.'

He moved carefully, trying not to dirty his beautifully polished shoes, treading the marshy path alongside a black ploughed field. When they came to a lane she held the strands of barbed wire wide for him so that he wouldn't tear his uniform. She herself would have liked to enter the wire on the opposite side of the road and tramp in a straight line across the grass towards the horizon and the dark row of houses before the sea-shore.

'Jesus,' he said with relief at standing on firm ground, and she stamped her foot at him.

'There's other words to use when you're cross. You don't have to say that.'

'Aw, come on, Rita.'

But she was striding off resentfully down the lane towards the corner where a red barn half-stood with its tin roof sliding into decay amidst a clump of elms. When he caught up with her he put his arm about her shoulders, but without warmth, digging his fingers into her flesh, shaking her. She became very still, waiting.

'What's up?'

'Nothing.'

'I guess your Auntie Margo wouldn't have no qualms about saying "Jesus". You're too sensitive getting all hotted up about a word.'

'Leave off.'

She shook herself free, pained that he had practically praised her aunt in preference to her, hearing the sound of marching feet beyond the barn and voices singing. She

52

pretended she was tying her shoelace, squatting down by the nettles and the ragged blackberry bushes, bowing her head. It was like being caught fraternising with the enemy, alone on a country road with an American. He lounged against the tangled hedge, sucking a blade of grass, watching the squad of soldiers stamping round the bend of the road, feet splayed out like Charlie Chaplin, stub-toed boots black as soot.

> My eyes are dim, I cannot see,
> I have not brought my specs with me ...

And a wail, drawn out, sorrowful, as if they howled in protest at walking through the warm afternoon :

> I have not brought
> My specs with me.

Ira whistled shrilly as they strutted past him, but he was ignored.

'Don't,' she hissed, crouching in the wet grass, fiddling with her shoe.

Eyes front, shoulders raised, they swung their arms and went mincing up the lane. The rooks left the elm trees and swooped down to the rusted roof of the empty barn.

'Don't,' she cried again, jumping upright and dragging on his arm as he stood blowing between his fingers in the middle of the lane. She wrenched his hands from his mouth, her face flushed with anger. 'Don't make a show of yourself.'

'What's got into you?' he wanted to know, digging his hands into his pockets and looking at her sullenly. Now that the soldiers had gone, she was sorry she had flared up at him.

'It's just that they don't like you, do they?'

'Who don't like me?' His eyes, grey not blue, reflecting the surface of the road, stared at her coldly.

'Our Tommies. They don't like the Yanks. It's the money you get.'

'We don't have no trouble with Tommies. We're allies.'

'Well,' she finished lamely, 'they have fights in Liverpool, down by Exchange Station. Everybody knows.'

'Is that so?' he muttered, turning from her and kicking at the hedgerow.

She didn't know how to remedy the situation. Rather like her Aunt Nellie who could never say she was sorry. She twisted her hands together and gazed helplessly at his hostile back.

'Oh,' she said, 'I didn't mean to speak out of turn.'

To her relief he stepped away from the hedge and shrugged his shoulders. But his face was hard. She looked at him furtively, trying to read his eyes, but they were guarded, revealing nothing.

'I'm sorry, Ira.'

Tears came to her eyes. He gave her a small lenient smile, and she was instantly restored, untroubled. The road led them toward the coast. They went along a cinder path over the railway and across another field.

'We could go home on the train,' she said, 'if we wanted.'

'I'm hungry,' he complained, but she didn't seem to hear him.

The land was level, the sky heaped with white cloud. She raced ahead of him between hedges inclined inwards against the constant wind blowing from the sea. They came to the long waste of foreshore and the row of empty houses heaped about with sand. He looked curiously at the deserted road and the front gardens run wild.

'Was this the blitz?' he asked.

She didn't know. 'It's near the docks and maybe people got scared and left. They don't look bombed.'

'They sure do,' he argued, looking at the windows empty of glass and the debris spilling on to the road.

'I think people are daft. I'd rather live here than Anfield.' And she ran into the nearest house, through the open doorway into a long hall that led into a back room overlooking the beach. 'Come on,' she shouted. 'It's nice in here.'

54

He followed her without enthusiasm, seeing the dog dirt on the floor and the human excrement and the soiled pieces of newspaper. Outside the window was a short garden with currant bushes and a broken wall tumbling down on to the sand.

Nellie had made her two sandwiches for her lunch and wrapped some biscuits. She took them out of her handbag and showed them to Ira. He held his hand out eagerly, but she put them away again, closing the clasp of her bag with a decisive little click.

'Later,' she said. 'I never have my dinner till one o'clock.'

It was a way she had with her, sticking to routine. They found strawberries in the garden, huddled under grey-green leaves weighted by sand. These at least she didn't own. She watched him as he strolled about the neglected garden, sitting on the faded square of lawn, and wished he would come near her. He leant against the crumbling wall looking at the barbed-wire entanglements rolling torn and rusted along the shore. In rows, the concrete bollards stood, planted to repel the landing craft.

'You don't talk much, do you?' she said, stung by his indifference.

'I guess I'm not much of a talker. Anyrate, I'm too hungry to think of words.'

She opened her handbag and took out the sandwiches and gave them to him. He lay down on his back full length upon the wall, tossing the paper wrapping on to the beach and holding the bread in both hands, his cap slipping sideways on to the grass. There was his ear, neat to his head and an inch of shaved scalp before his bleached hair began.

'Your Auntie Margo make you these?' he munched.

'Never,' she scoffed. 'She wouldn't give you the time of day.'

She felt uncomfortable being mean about Auntie Margo, and she could hardly credit that what she felt was jealousy.

55

'Auntie Margo isn't much good at shopping and stuff. Nellie does all that.'

'Did you tell your auntie that you were meeting me?'

'I didn't like.'

'Don't they let you date?'

'I don't talk to them very much.'

He didn't comment. He folded his arms behind his head and closed his eyes.

After a while she opened her bag and took out mother's pearl beads and laid them on the grass. She looked round for something to dig in the soil, something sharp. In time, she found the jagged half of a slate fallen from the roof, and she knelt and scooped a hole in the sandy earth. When she was ready, she put the beads in the shallow depression and spooned the sand back into place. Finally, she threw the slate over the wall into the next garden and stamped the ground level with her shoes. She snapped a piece from the flowering currant bush growing by the wall and planted it on the spot where she had buried the necklace. Wiping her hand on her coat, she went and looked down at his face. His eyelids quivered.

'You're shamming,' she said. 'You're never sleeping.'

There was a line of sweat beading his upper lip and the dull gleam of a tooth where his mouth lay slack. She shook him gently and felt his body tense so that he wouldn't fall off the wall.

'What were you putting in the earth?'

'Secret. Mind your own business.'

He sat up then and shook her quite roughly by the shoulders, thrusting his narrow face at her. Suddenly he kissed her. So flat and hard her gums ached. She pulled away from his mouth and buried her face in his jacket to hide her wide smile of delight that it had happened at last. He swung her round and stood holding her by the hips, pushing himself against her. All her bones hurt and the top of her legs where the broken wall caught her. But it didn't matter. Possession blazed up in her, consuming : someone belonged to her. After the war he would take her to the States, and they'd have a long black car and a grand piano with a bowl of flowers on the lid. There'd be a house with a verandah and wooden steps, and she would run down them in a dress with lots of folds in the skirt and peep-toed shoes. Auntie Nellie would tell Mrs Mander how well-off they were, how Ira cared for her, the promotion he kept getting at work.

'What you say?' he asked, flushed in the face.

'What's your work when you're not a soldier?'

He was clutching her hair in two bunches on either side of her head, tilting her neck. Her mouth opened like a fish.

'You're hurting me.'

He let go at once, taking a step backwards, and she followed him blindly, nestling up to him, content to be on a level with his chest, her arms rather awkwardly about him, her head full of dreams.

'What job do you do when you're not in the army?'

'I ain't got no job. Leastways, nothing settled.'

He was bringing his arm up against her chest as if to push her away but his fingers were feeling the fabric of her dress.

'Leave off!' she cried, shocked, butting him with her head so that he stumbled and almost fell.

'You shouldn't do things like that. It's rude doing that.'

Already she was wishing he was different, more to her liking – more chatty, ask her things, tell her about the future, kiss her gently on the lips and not act rude.

He sat down on the wall, defeated, and scratched his head. She felt scorn for him because he didn't know how to behave. And yet she did love him. She went clumsily and put her arms about his neck, pushing his head down against the throat of her dress, stroking the skin behind his ear as if he was the cat.

'I like kissing,' she said primly, 'but I don't want to do anything rude.'

'I can't make you out,' he said. 'I don't see what I done that was rude.'

57

The tide was coming in, the sea invading the beach, trickling through the line of concrete defences. She patted his back, as if he was a child that had fallen over.

'I don't think it was very awful,' she said, helplessly. But he laced his arms slackly about her waist and did not attempt to kiss her again.

They walked to the nearest railway station to catch a train to the town. There was a public house near the ticket office and he wanted to see if he could get a drink, but she said her Auntie Nellie wouldn't like it. She hung on his arm and chattered all the time, filled with confidence, sitting on the upholstered railway seat with her torn stockings and her muddy shoes stretched out for all to see. She covered his hand with both her own, like a little dry animal she was keeping from running away.

# 5

JACK came to take them for a run in the car.

'One of these days,' warned Nellie darkly and left the room to fetch her coat.

'Don't you want a run out?' he asked when she returned, but she drew in her narrow lips and kept silent.

'I'm allowed a certain amount of petrol,' he said mildly.

'It's not right, Jack, and you know it, buying black-market stuff.'

'Good God, woman!' he exploded. 'Anyone would think I was the Gauleiter of Anfield, plundering the poor.' He felt quite nettled and put out.

'Take no notice,' said Margo, and told Rita to get her things on.

Nellie sat on the front seat beside him and he wound a rug about her knees. It was raining and the streets were gloomy; he didn't know where to go.

'Do you fancy anywhere special?' he asked Nellie, driving down Breck Road towards the cemetery and turning into Prescott Avenue. He would have suggested a cup of tea at Winifred's Cottage on the East Lancs road, but it was a fair run and he didn't want another scene over his petrol ration.

'I want to go to the Cathedral,' said Rita, tapping his shoulder.

She was wearing some kind of scent, sweet and powerful.

'My word, someone smells nice. Doesn't she smell nice, Auntie Nellie?'

59

But Nellie only nodded her head with an air of martydom, and Marge remarked grimly from the back seat: 'You'll not get a word out of her. She's been like Sarah Bernhardt all week.'

He thought maybe that Nellie had been overdoing it, that she needed a holiday. When she put her hat on, he had noticed the pallor of her face and a little blue vein standing out on her forehead. But where could the girls go for a holiday, that was the problem. Most of the seaside boarding houses had been requisitioned, and he doubted if Marge could get off work.

'Nellie, what was that place we went to in Shropshire before the war?'

Rita said: 'I don't want to be late back, Uncle Jack. I'm going out later.'

'What place?' asked Nellie.

'It had a bowling green. When they put a net up it was a tennis court. You remember.'

'Herbert Arms Hotel,' said Margo. 'Where are you going, Rita?'

'Just out.'

'That's right, Marge, the Herbert Arms. Everybody round a big table for meals and there was a yard with a stable.' He hardly saw the familiar streets for the picture in his mind of a grey church and an old car parked near a bridge. They had jam for tea in little bowls, all different kinds – strawberry and plum and blackcurrant jelly.

'It was a cow shed,' said Marge, 'with cows, and a great big hill of muck outside the back door.'

'Trust you to remember that,' said Nellie.

'Get off!' Jack said. 'It was a proper midden, scientific. There was no smell. They put it on the fields.'

They were driving up Princes Road toward the Park, overtaking a solitary tram. The tall trees in the centre of the boulevard were heavy with rain. They swayed and dripped, turning the interior of the van into a green box full of shadows.

60

Marge was laughing in the back of the car. Jack looked in the mirror and saw her wiping her eyes with her handkerchief.

'What's up with you, Marge?'

'I just thought of that chappie from the Wirral with the short pants.'

'The what?'

'With the bike.'

'It was a tandem,' said Nellie, and her lips curved upward at the corner and she let out a little abrupt snigger.

'By heck,' said Jack delightedly, 'I'd forgotten him. With red hair –'

'And his mam rubbed his legs with goose fat to keep them ready for his bike –'

They were all laughing now, thinking of Marge going off on the tandem with him in little short white socks and a pair of tennis pumps. It was funny, Jack thought, how Marge always attracted the men, even if they were silly beggars. She always had, even when she was getting past her prime. And he darted a quick look into the mirror and saw her there, with tears running down her face and her two cheeks flushed with rouge and her body the same thickness from shoulder to thigh.

They went down hill towards the river. Passing the old black houses built by the shipping owners, four-storeys high with pillars at the front door and steps of granite – occupied now by riff-raff : washing hung sodden on the wrought-iron balconies, a pram with three wheels in the gutter, a running herd of children without shoes. Some of the railings had been taken away to be melted down for the war-effort and there was wire meshing to stop people breaking their necks in the blackout. There was the new Cathedral rising like an ocean liner out of the sunken graveyard, tethered to its dry dock by giant cranes, coloured all over a soft and rusty pink. Rita wouldn't let him take her round to the front entrance. They parked on Hope Street and watched her push her way through a portion of broken fencing into the cemetery.

'Why can't she use the proper gate?' asked Margo.

'I wouldn't mind going for a walk down there myself,' Jack said, and he looked sideways at Nellie. 'Do you feel like a blow?'

'It's drizzling. Let the child be on her own. It's natural. She doesn't want you lumbering about after her.'

'Would you like a holiday?' he asked after a while. He opened the window to let out the smoke from Marge's cigarette. She looked at him astonished. 'You've been looking peaky lately,' he said.

'How can I go on a holiday with young Rita to look after?'

'Well, there's Marge —'

She withered him with a glance. 'I wouldn't leave the cat with our Marge,' she said.

'By heck, I'd take a damn sight more care of her than you do.'

There was a silence while the storm gathererd.

Jack looked out of the window and saw the small figure moving along the path that wound round the walls, descending lower into the well of the cemetery. She stopped to pull leaves from a bush. On the sky-line floated one small barrage balloon, idiotic, like something a kiddie had drawn with a blue crayon.

'That would be a fat lot of good,' he said, half to himself. Marge was going on and on in that way she had, stumbling over her words. She had a good voice, throaty – not like Nellie's, strained and shrill. Whatever Nellie said came out like a criticism because of the lack of tone.

Marge said: 'She said she was going out tonight. You never asked her where.'

'I know where, that's why.'

'Well, where is she going?'

'She's going to the moving pictures with Cissie Baines,' Nellie said grudgingly.

'Well, she might say that, but you can't be sure.'

'Get away with you!' Nellie said, twisting round in her

seat to look at Marge. 'D'you know what, Miss? I think you're jealous, you're blooming jealous.'

Jack tried to keep out of it. In a way it was easy, for he had heard of it all before, not the same subject, but the bitterness lying beneath the words. Nobody could keep young Rita chained up. If she said she was going out with Cissie Baines he supposed she was. Marge wanted to know if it was Cissie Baines she had gone out with earlier in the week and come home with her stockings in a mess and her shoes all muddy. Jack wondered if the parents of Cissie were arguing about Rita at this moment.

'We don't even know who Cissie Baines is,' cried Margo. 'We've never set eyes on her. We don't know where she lives or if she's rough or anything.'

He could see Rita leaping about the path far below. She wore a macintosh and a spotted scarf wound round her head. Beyond the river he thought he could make out the distant blue swell of the Cheshire hills. The voices went on around him, Marge attacking, Nellie defending. Sooner or later Marge would go too far and Nellie would take umbrage and they'd have a silent drive back and a silent tea of cold meat that he'd brought and half a tomato each. The thought of the little bowls of jam on the white cloth years ago nagged him.

'D'you remember the plum jam,' he said unwisely, 'and the crab apple jelly?' His face was illuminated, his eyes round with longing under the shabby Homburg hat.

'If I told you,' said Margo, rounding on him in fury, 'that your Rita was nicking things, I don't suppose you'd take a blind bit of notice.'

'Steady on!' he said, sobered. 'What d'you mean, Marge?' He looked at Nellie for an explanation.

'Take no notice. She's touched.'

'No, no, steady on.' He was insistent. 'What she mean by that?'

'She's lost that necklace and some book she had in a drawer.'

'What necklace?'

'That necklace I put on to go to Valerie Mander's the other night. It's gone,' said Margo dramatically.

'The state you came home in that night it's a wonder you brought your clothes home, never mind a string of beads,' snapped Nellie.

'You grudge my going out, you do. You'd like me locked indoors pedalling away on a sewing machine and me mouth jammed full of pins. You'd like to keep me down –'

'Keep you down!' Nellie gave a little sarcastic laugh. 'Who blacked the grate every morning of their life and who left me to nurse Mother and Uncle Wilf?'

'You wouldn't let me see him,' wailed Margo, her eyes glittering, remembering George Bickerton dying upstairs.

Jack was trying to fathom what it had to do with Rita. They goaded each other with memories of the past and confused him with their bickering.

'You stopped me going to the keep-fit classes,' cried Margo.

'I never –'

'You rang up the fire-post behind me back and told them I was too poorly to fire-watch any more –'

They were spitting at each other like cats, arching their necks and clawing at the leather seating of the car.

Below in the cemetery Rita meandered between laurel and dusty rhododendron and frail spires of mountain ash.

'By God!' began Nellie, and he turned to look at her and watched her eyes open very wide as if she saw something outside on the road that surprised her. Above the little white muffler tucked about her neck her lips were turning a delicate shade of violet.

'Hey-up, Nellie!' he cried in alarm, as she slid downwards in her seat and fluttered her eyes. He couldn't think what to do at first. Marge said it was sheer bad temper that made her go off in a faint. 'Shut your gob!' he shouted, out of his mind with fright, because he knew it was her heart.

He got out of the car and half-laid her across the two front

64

seats, taking his coat off and bundling it under her head. Something about her thick little ankles and the sensible shoes like boots he had worn as a boy caught in his throat. He tried to call Rita to come quickly, but the wind pulled his voice and she didn't look round. He looked for a house so that he could get help, but there was only a row of half-demolished buildings on the far side of the road and he didn't like to leave Nellie alone with Marge, who was crying now.

'It's your heart,' he muttered, kneeling on the running board of the van and patting Nellie's gloved hand so that she would know he was near.

'Go and get Rita,' he ordered Marge, wanting to get the sick woman home and in her bed.

After a moment Nellie opened her eyes and he told her to lie still. He looked back and he could see Marge running along the edge of the fencing waving her arms and shouting 'Rita!' A small girl came with great patches of hair missing from her head and stared into the van without expression.

'It's your heart,' he told Nellie, over and over, for he wanted to reassure her that it wasn't a road accident or a nightmare or something she couldn't understand.

He gritted his teeth and prayed for Rita to hurry up. Marge was still swooping up and down the fence, like some gull crying in the wind. Nellie was conscious now, a little more composed. Struggling to sit up, she tried to ram her hat more securely on to her head.

'Look at your good coat,' she said weakly, and he flapped it straight and put it over her and the rug on top of that.

Rita and he put her to bed when they got home, taking her out of her tight dress and leaving her in her slip and her corsets. Marge went up the road to the Manders to use their telephone to send for Dr Bogle. To Rita, the house was exciting, full of whisperings and sudden knocks at the door.

'She does too much,' said Jack for the umpteenth time, striding back and forth with his hat still on his head, waiting for Dr Bogle to finish his examination.

65

Nellie was quiet enough when Dr Bogle had gone. She liked him : he was her generation, he never asked too many questions. He told her she should lie up for a day or two and not fret about the house.

'After all,' he said without malice, 'it'll still be here after you're gone.'

He went downstairs to talk to Jack and left her moping in the chill little bedroom with the rain sliding down the window. She decided she would do as she was told, stay in her bed for a day or two and Marge could take time off work and keep house and make her a cup of tea when required. She needed time to think what she was going to do about the future. Marge had been right when she had cried out to Jack in the van that it was bad temper had had made her turn dizzy. It had come on when Marge had accused her of stopping her from attending the keep-fit classes. It was a lie, and the anger she felt at Marge twisting the facts to suit herself had risen in her like bile, choking her. She would have to find some way of detaching herself from such irritations, until she had worked out what to do with the furniture. Rita would have to find a young man and settle down. Jack could find them a house somewhere, nothing fancy, and the sideboard and the sofa and chairs and the bone china could be moved there, into the best front room, away from Marge and her slatternly ways. For the moment she would suggest as quietly as possible that Marge keep her underwear clean until she was up and about again, and pray to God that she wouldn't be run over by a tram before she herself was fit to do the washing.

Margo was very chastened, the fire gone out of her. She didn't even say much when Rita said she was off out if nobody needed her. Jack gave her a ten-shilling note and told her to be a good girl.

'Oh, I wish I hadn't argued with Nellie,' said Margo, when they were alone.

'You've got a vicious tongue in your head, Marge. Mind

66

you, she's not the easiest of women to get on with. She's a good woman, and they're the worst.'

He sat dangling his small hands between his knees, sitting on Nellie's chair beside the grate. Bogle had said there wasn't much to worry about, it was only a little warning that she should take it easy. It would be best in future not to upset her, not to cause scenes likely to bring on an attack.

'How long has she been moody?' he asked Marge; and she replied more or less since the beginning of the week when she'd gone to a friend after work and not come straight home. Nellie said she'd get her ciggies for her, only she forgot; and when Marge spoke out of turn Nellie flew up in a paddy and had hardly uttered a civil word since.

'Ah well,' he said and turned on the wireless to relieve the gloom.

He made Nellie a cup of cocoa, but she didn't want it, and he brought it downstairs and drank it himself. Though there was still daylight outside the window, inside the kitchen it had grown dark. The dimensions of the room were mean, depressing without the glow of a fire. All the good furniture had been removed into the front room – dining-room table, sideboard, the oak chair that father had sat in. Nellie had replaced them with cheap utility stuff bought at Lewis's.

'By heck,' he said, 'I'll get the electric put in before another winter passes.'

'She won't like that,' said Margo. 'You know what she's like about the house being shook up.'

Jack went and lit the oven in the scullery for warmth. Margo sat in her coat feeling sorry for herself; the sausage curls above her ears hung bedraggled from all her running about in the rain. Jack put the tea on the table but neither of them felt up to eating.

'I'm that cold,' he complained, standing up at the table, hugging himself with his arms.

About his brow was a red mark where the band of his hat had bitten too tight. If the calendar said it was summer, even

67

if there was snow on the wash-house roof, Nellie wouldn't light a fire. She said they needed the coal for the winter. In vain he told her that things were going to get better, now the Allies had landed in Europe. She'd read of people being extravagant and having to burn the furniture to stop themselves from freezing to death.

Some lady on the wireless was singing a song about Tomorrow When the World was Free :

> There'll be blue birds over
> The white cliffs of Dover
> Tomorrow just you wait and see . . .

He joined in the chorus, but his voice broke with emotion and he cleared his throat several times to get over it. Margo was watching him with contemptuous eyes.

'It's something to do with the word,' he said. 'It always chokes me up.'

'What word, you soft beggar?'

'Blue.' He emptied his nose vigorously into his handkerchief. 'I remember a bit of poetry at St Emmanuel's, something about the old blue faded flower of day.'

'Oh yes,' she said, mocking him.

'And there's bluebird, bluebell –'

'Blue-bottle,' said Marge, and he had to laugh.

There was a great storm of applause on the wireless to greet the end of the song. They both glanced up at the ceiling, hoping Nellie wouldn't think they were making a holy show of themselves.

When it was quite dark in the kitchen he went again up the stairs and whispered : 'Nellie, Nellie, anything you want?'

She didn't reply. He tip-toed to her bed and she was lying with her hand tucked under her cheek, her body tidy under the counterpane – beneath the bed, half peeping, her shoes with the laces spread.

\*      \*      \*

There was a row of women standing in front of the long mirror in the ladies' waiting room, spitting into little boxes and stabbing eye-black on their lashes. Uncle Jack said they came from all over England, hitch-hiking, making for the American army bases. He said they were mad for the money the Yanks threw about. 'They're wicked women,' he said, spitting the words out through puritanical lips, and Rita had believed him. But she knew better now : it wasn't the money, it was a search for love, the sort she had found with Ira. The women looked common enough with their bleached hair and their mouths pouting as they put on lipstick, but they weren't wicked.

' 'Scuse me,' she said politely, edging her way in and resting her handbag on the ledge.

Her head scarf was saturated with the rain. Underneath, her hair was limp, crushed to her skull as if oiled. There was a girl with a paper bag full of sand, one leg on the leather seating of the bench. She was rubbing the yellow grains into her skin trying to simulate stockings. The sand fell in a little heap to the floor. Rita wiped her face with a handkerchief and squeezed Creme Simone on to her nose and her cheeks. She had found the cream and a box of orange powder in Auntie Marge's drawer, but there wasn't a powder puff. Carefully she dipped the end of her hankie into the box and dabbed it on her face. When she was finished she didn't know that she liked herself. If her hair would only dry it would give her a softer look, less exposed.

Ira wasn't outside, under the clock, as they had arranged, but then it was raining and he was possibly near the taxi rank or by the barrier, or in the main hall, or the lavatory, combing his hair to look nice for her. She looked everywhere and stood outside the Gentlemen's convenience for almost ten minutes until a sailor came out, with his collar flapping upwards behind his head like a blue sail, and stared at her as if he knew her. He was small and quite old and she didn't want Ira to see her with him – he might think she was man-

69

crazy. She went back into the waiting-room and sat down. There was a different batch of women, newly arrived off the Warrington train. They slumped dishevelled on the black-leather seating, smoking cigarettes, chewing gum. There was a woman that reminded her of Aunt Nellie : the droop to the mouth, the expression in her eyes beneath a tangle of wet black hair. She wore a bow of crumpled white satin, one end hanging forlornly over her plucked eyebrow. She never took her eyes off Rita, not even when children ran in screaming through the open doorway, banging sticks on the oil-cloth of the centre table. When they rolled on the floor, Rita could see the marks of insect bites, pin-points of scarlet clear up the thin legs to the gape of their torn knickers. She could smell the children : a mixture of damp old clothing and dirt, and something sickly like the stored grain in the warehouses; and she sat quite still with one hand curled into a fist as the lavatory lady ran in from the wash-room and ordered them out.

The woman with the bow in her hair made Rita feel uncomfortable. She imagined that it was written all over her face that she had found someone to love her, that she had Ira. She longed for him to come to the door and call her name and she would run to him and all the tired and mucky women on the benches would realise she was different from them. But he didn't come, and after a while she walked out into the station, which was crowded now with soldiers and airman and shrieking women, for the trains ran too and fro between the American base outside Warrington and the army barracks at Freshfield and the aerodrome at Woodvale. The military police patrolled in pairs, swaggering in their white helmets, swinging their truncheons from their wrists on little bands of leather. She went down the steps past the taxi-rank under the arch of the station entrance into Stanley Street. For a time she stood in the doorway of the philately shop, sheltered from the rain, absorbed in a page of German stamps imprinted with Hitler's head. But for him, she thought, she would never have met Ira, never been happy. Uncle Jack said he was a maniac, the monster of the world. She thought he looked rather neat and gentlemanly with his smart black tie and his hair slicked down over one eye. Now and then she popped her head out of the doorway and stared down the road at the station. She went lower down the street to the chemists, looking at all the funny objects in the window: rubber trusses and surgical braces and adverts for pills and lotions. There was a photograph of a man in his combs flexing his muscles like a boxer. There was a great brown nozzle with a ball at one end and holes in the head. 'Whirling Spray,' she read, but there was nothing to say what it was for. It was too big for an ear syringe. She supposed it was for something rude, like the things described in Auntie Marge's hidden book. She didn't like to be seen staring into the window, and there was a tiny sensation of fright just beginning to grow somewhere in her head or her heart. Why hadn't he come yet? Please God, she prayed, don't let him be dead. Make it be the right place and the right day. Bending her head against the gusts of rain she walked back to the station. He was there, lounging against the soot-covered wall under the giant wrought-iron clock.

'Oh,' she cried, laughing with relief, 'I was beginning to think –'

'The train was late. The guard wouldn't shift till some of the guys got out of the carriage.'

He didn't attempt to kiss her cheek, but she was too grateful at his arrival to be discouraged. She did recognise that some part of him resisted her. She saw in his cool untroubled eyes an absence of warmth as if he didn't realise that he had been waiting all his life to find her. He was slow and unaware, locked in the protracted torpor of adolescence.

'We can go to the movies,' he said, looking at her rain-soaked clothes and her face yellow with powder.

'I can't go to the flicks now. It's too late. I can't be late home – me Auntie Nellie's poorly.'

She loved walking with him, holding his arm. She hardly

71

noticed the rain or how cold it had grown. In her head they spoke to one another tenderly, talking about the future, how they loved each other, moving through the town, he with his coat collar turned up against the wind, she with her head scarf trailing about her shoulders – arm in arm, completely silent in the Double Summertime. They walked almost to the Pier Head, sheltering under the black arch of the overhead railway that ran alongside the docks.

'Is it like home?' she wanted to know, listening to the sound of a train rumbling above them, thinking it was like a film she'd seen about America. The municipal gardens in front of the Pier were deserted. The green benches dripped water. Spray rose above the river wall and blew like smoke across the bushes and the grass.

'It ain't nothing like home,' he said.

They walked back to the town, thankful to have the wind behind them.

'Don't you wish we were in the country again?' she asked, but he didn't answer : he wouldn't commit himself. If it had been the aunt's, she would have taken the silence for moodiness. But he, she knew, used words sparingly. When the time came he would know how to talk to her. There were numerous bars and cafés, but she didn't want to share him, nor did she think Auntie Nellie would approve of such places.

'We ought to shelter from the rain,' he said. 'I guess you're soaked right through.'

'I don't mind,' she said truthfully, and he stopped quite still and touched the shoulder of her macintosh. 'You sure feel like a drowned rat.'

She stopped breathing with the hurt, blinking her eyes, not knowing where to look. Everything was suddenly cold and bleak, the black buildings rising into the grey sky, the street filled with strangers wrapped in one another's arms.

'I've got to get my tram now,' she said, and in her head he pleaded with her : Please don't leave me now – you're pretty as a picture, you're lovely as a rose garden.

72

They waited in the tram shelter outside Owen Owen's and she studied the angle of his jaw as he turned to listen to the music of a dance band from the Forces Club across the street. When she boarded the tram he waved his hand in farewell, and she sat stiffly, holding her handbag to her chest, watching him for one brief moment as he sprinted across the street, before the tram clanged its bell and tore her from him.

# 6

---

R ITA was in the first stage of her nightmare. As yet she had made no sound. She lay perfectly flat with her hands outside the sheets.

She was in the back of the Wolsely car, the green card table in position . . . They were driving down the long road of detached houses. Early evening . . . she looked through the glass at the gardens. The silver lamp post . . . the stretch of fencing . . . now the house. Windows closed to the air . . . the wire basket full of lobelia hanging from the roof of the porch. Inside were the people she cared for . . . never seen . . . they sat somewhere inside on high polished chairs. In the upstairs window a plaster girl patting the ears of a dog with a feathery tail . . . sweet peas cut from the garden in a bowl on the hall table . . . grandfather clock with the hands at eight o'clock . . . a statue in bronze of two men wrestling with an angel . . . a row of tins on the pantry shelf, salmon, soup, pears. A round window cut like a porthole in the front door . . . a little frilly skirt of curtain . . . they passed the house and drove into darkness.

She stirred in the bed, brought her arm up over her face.

She was watching the sky roll down into place at the end of the road. The painted poplars straightened and stood still. The engine of the car ticked over . . . waiting . . . the red

74

penny sun slid into view . . . she tapped the glass partition with a little stick . . . the car drove slowly toward the fence. The house deserted . . . the people gone away on holiday . . . the locks broken on the door . . . the garden gate swinging. Silver gone from the sideboard . . . knives ripped from the green baize box . . . decanters of cut glass torn from the back of the dark cupboard . . . the statue of the naked men toppled from its stand . . . jewellery missing from the upstairs room . . . the good diamond ring, the watch with the platinum bracelet, the glass beads from Venice. And a hat with a pin, speared like a roasting chicken on the banister rail in the hall.

She almost woke now, she tried, she fought to get out of the darkness, opening her mouth and beginning to whimper.

The car crawled to the edge of the kerb . . . slowed to a halt beyond the silver lamp post . . . out on the front lawn among the dahlias the pieces of furniture . . . the polished chairs . . . the grandfather clock . . . the wrestling men flashing fire from the sun . . . a body flung like a doll among the sweet williams . . . a man hanging over the fence with his head dripping blood . . . the people she knew . . . the loved ones . . .

She screamed, trying to get out of the bed, drowning in waves of sleep. A long moment of pressure, heart beating, the blood pounding in her ears, dizzy like a heat wave.

'It's alright our Rita, it's alright Lamb, hush up our Rita, it's alright.'

She woke, trying to focus the dark cold bedroom, seeing the dull cylinders of Margo's curlers touched by a rind of light at the window.

'I can't,' she said. 'It's not my fault.'

\*     \*     \*

When Nellic had recovered, she made one or two adjust-

75

ments to the front room. She moved upstairs to the box-room the little rosewood table and the china figure of a rustic boy resting his chin on his hand. She would have liked to store the sideboard too, but she felt Marge would notice, and it was too heavy to shift without help. She wasn't entirely sure in her mind why it was important to make such a change, to disturb articles of furniture that had taken up their allotted space in the best front room for so many years – whether it was to decrease their chance of decay or to test her reaction to the disappearance of familiar objects. Either way she felt that she had accomplished something. Apart from the truckle bed that had always been there, the box-room, though small, could accommodate other pieces: the shelved mirror with the curved frame, the foot-stool embroidered in faded silks, the bamboo stand which displayed the aspidistra plant. She fully intended to remove all these items – gradually, so as not to cause comment, over a period of months. And to help Rita to find a nice young man and settle down she would make her a whole new wardrobe of clothes, dresses for the winter, a costume, a new coat with a fur collar. She had expected the child to be less than enthusiastic, but she seemed to welcome the suggestion. She spent several evenings poring over pattern books looking for ideas. Jack was astonished when Nellie asked him if he could lay his hands on some extra clothing coupons. Rita said she would go with Nellie to Birkenhead market to choose material, but it would have to be early on the Saturday.

'I suppose you're off out in the evening,' said Margo.

'Yes, I am.'

'With Cissie Baines, I expect,' said Margo sarcastically, but the child only nodded her head passively and went on turning the pages of a book.

They took the mid-day ferry from the Pier Head, leaving Margo at home to do the shopping. She didn't argue. She dreaded lest she should upset Nellie and be forced to spend another few days washing the pots and cooking the meagre scraps of food.

Rita went upstairs on deck while Nellie made herself comfortable in the saloon, sinking into the dimpling black leather of the seats that lined the wall, following the curve of the boat. She wriggled herself backwards into position, as if she sat in a dentist's chair, her feet not quite touching the floor, with a clear view of the Pier Head and the gulls gliding outside the glass. She liked the throb of the engines beneath her, the low whine of agony as the boat shuddered and chaffed the rope buffers of the landing stage, the gush of tumbled water as it moved backwards and swung in a wide circle to face the opposite side of the river. There were brave souls marching the deck: a student from the university with his scarf blowing in the air behind him like a woolly streamer, a man clamping his hands to his head as the wind tore at his trilby hat.

It reminded her of the time Jack had sent them to Ireland for a holiday. He'd paid for it. He knew some hotel outside Dublin that he'd been to years ago at the time of the Black and Tans, but he couldn't afford for them to have a cabin and she'd sat up all night on deck under a tarpaulin, with little Rita asleep on her lap – everyone moaning as the ship rolled, for all the world as if they were immigrants on their way to America. They went on a train along the coast and at the station there were some taxis and a funny old-fashioned carriage drawn by horses. And there was Marge, the daft beggar, bustling past the ordinary vehicles and bundling them into the buggy cart, driving through the streets to the hotel, swaying and bouncing, making a right show of themselves. It was a lovely holiday. It was nice to watch Rita running in and out of the waves with her little dress tucked into her knickers. Of course, Marge made a fool of herself, getting off with a commercial traveller from Birmingham, saying she was going off on the bus to Bray, and her and Rita walking past a café in the afternoon and seeing Marge and him sitting in the the window eating egg-and-cress sandwiches: caught red-handed in a yellow straw-hat with red roses on the brim and a piece of watercress stuck to her lip.

Rita searched for Nellie as the bell clanged for the passengers to disembark. Through the window of the saloon she saw her aunt's corpse-like face etched on the darkness of the interior. She was smiling with her eyes closed, as if she was happy, the clasped hands on her lap threaded through the strings of her shopping bag. Rita tapped on the glass. Nellie opened her eyes immediately, stared uncertainly, then came in a little unsteady run to the swing doors, clasping the brass rail for support.

'My word it's rough,' she said. 'You look like the Wreck of the Hesperus.'

She hadn't been to Birkenhead for two years and was appalled at the change: the air of decay and obliteration. The municipal gardens were laid to waste. Gone were the roses and the shrubs, the drinking fountain with its marble basin – nothing now but two slopes of sparse grass; the railings carted away; dogs doing their business where once the tulips had swayed in scarlet ranks.

Rita wanted black worsted for a dress. She didn't care what else, but she wanted the black.

'It's a bit old,' said Nellie.

'I want pleats in the skirt and a white collar and white cuffs.'

'Sure you don't want some lace for a frilly cap and apron?' said Nellie tartly. 'Then we could get you a job in the Kardomah.'

But Rita insisted. Nellie bought four yards of black, five of grey with a stripe in it and a piece of pink velvet.

They had a cup of tea standing up at a stall and Rita wanted to buy a meat pie.

'You won't, Miss,' said Nellie.

'It's me own money.'

'No.'

Nellie had always impressed on both Rita and Marge that there were two things they must never do: never sit down on somebody else's lav and never eat a shop-bought meat pie.

78

The girl seemed to go into a sulk. On her face a look of suffering as if she had been mortally wounded. She stood there, her face shut to all approaches. Only her eyes were alive, watching the crowd of shoppers in the market square with a peculiar intensity, as if she was searching for someone.

*     *     *

Mrs Mander told Margo that things had grown very serious between Chuck and Valerie. There just might be an engagement announcement soon. It would mean a new dress for Valerie if Nellie was up to it. Something romantic, embroidered with sequins to catch the light. She found the ravaged interest of Margo's expression disconcerting : she looked like a woman gutted by fire – she was wearing a dress of a slightly charred texture, several sizes too large for her, with panels of silver let into the bodice. There was a scorch mark at the shoulder and a diamante clasp at the hip. Her fatigued eyes glittered with excitement as she told Mrs Mander how thrilled she was for Valerie. In the fulfilment of the girl's dreams she imagined that she herself moved one step nearer to happiness. Nellie would make the dress, she was sure – why, no one could stop her. She lit a cigarette with trembling fingers and went to fetch the pattern books from under the stairs so that they could begin at once their search for the ideal gown. Forgotten were the preparations for the evening meal, and Mrs Mander was too polite to say it was Nellie's opinion she had come for, even though Marge was younger and could be said to be more modern in her outlook. There were certain indications of hysteria in Marge's appearance, a lack of judgment : the cocktail dress in which she had answered the door, the fur coat she wore to work with white wedge-heeled shoes. There was the occasion, never to be forgotten, when the Dutch seaman billeted on them in the first year of the war had given her a length of cloth from the East and she had gone secretly

79

behind Nellie's back and had it made up into a sarong – wearing it at a Women's Guild night, with a slit right up the leg and all her suspenders showing beneath the baggy edge of her green silk drawers.

'Nellie's gone to get material for Rita from Birkenhead market. She's suddenly taken an interest in clothes,' said Margo.

'Well, she would, wouldn't she?' said Mrs Mander. 'Valerie says she's started courting. She saw them down town last Saturday.'

Margo stared at her. Once her mouth moved perceptibly, as if she was about to say something, but no words came; she wet her dry lips with her tongue. Mrs Mander was busy studying a three-quarter length dress with a little matching bolero.

'It's nice,' she said. 'We could put sequins on the coatee.' She looked up sharply and asked: 'What do you think of him?'

'Well, we hardly know him – she's only been going out with him a short time.' She prayed she was accurate, that Mrs Mander wouldn't catch on.

'Well, you spoke to him at our house.'

'What did you make of him?' asked Margo, stalling for time, trying to remember which young man in particular Rita had sat with. It could only be the fellow in the wardrobe, the long bony lad with the big feet. She felt enormous relief at being able to visualise him – that it wasn't some unknown brutal stranger doing nasty things to Rita.

'Valerie says her Chuck doesn't know him very well. He came along that night because he'd been seeing to Chuck's jeep.'

She implied, Margo felt, that he was in some way inferior to Chuck, less of a catch.

'He's a nice lad,' said Margo. 'Very polite. He knows his manners. His father's got quite a business in the city.'

'What city?' asked Mrs Mander mercilessly and Margo

said it was Washington, near the White House, and was afraid she had made a fool of herself and that the White House was actually in New York.

'That's nice,' said Mrs Mander. 'You know, with the lovely figure our Valerie's got, it's a crying shame to have a jacket.'

'That's true,' Margo said, and wished she would go away quickly before too many things were said. She had known all along that Rita was being secretive, coming home with her stockings ripped to pieces and going down town on a Saturday night and returning drenched to the skin and worn out. That's why she'd had her nightmare. The deceit had preyed on her mind. She herself had tried to keep things from Nellie all her life. She didn't blame Rita, but she was hurt that the girl hadn't confided in her. She felt resentful to be shut out from excitement and intrigue. She had tried in her fashion to shield Rita from Nellie's influence, to add a little gaiety to the narrow years spent in the narrow house.

'I'll take the books back with me,' said Mrs Mander. 'Tell Nellie I called.'

And she was off out through the door rushing back to the lovely Valerie to tell her that Rita hadn't let on at home she was meeting a soldier.

*     *     *

Margo might have told Jack if she had known more herself about the lad in the wardrobe. She longed to be able to tell him that Rita had confided in her. It would make her seem mature in Jack's eyes : it was always to Nellie that he turned for advice.

Jack kept complaining of a stomach ache. Nellie made him a glass of hot water to sip before going up the road to congratulate Valerie.

'Are you going now?' asked Margo, alarmed. She didn't want Mrs Mander blurting it all out to Nellie.

'If I have your permission,' said Nellie sharply, tucking her hair under her hat.

'Don't you think,' said Margo, when Nellie had gone, 'that we had a rum childhood – I mean, thinking about it –'

'Rum,' said Jack, not understanding.

'Restricted. The way Mother was – all them rules, going to church.'

'What rules?'

'Don't you think we were damaged?'

'Don't talk daft.'

He sat up, clutching his belly, filled with irritation at the way she carried on. Whenever Marge started to talk in this fashion it made him angry : he was defending someone, something, but he didn't know what. It was like when Lord Haw Haw had been on the wireless – he wanted to jump to his feet and wave the flag.

'We were never given a chance,' said Margo. 'Never. All that church-going and being respectable – you can never get away from it.'

'Church never did anyone any harm,' he said hotly.

'You haven't been inside a church for donkey's years.'

'It never did any harm,' he repeated doggedly. 'It might have been better if you had listened to what the good book said.'

'I did listen – I did nothing else. Always being told what to do, always being got at. Doing what Mother said was best.'

'Mother was a wonderful woman,' he cried, looking at her with hostility. 'She brought us up never to owe a penny, never to ask anybody for anything.'

'She asked Nellie for plenty. It was Nellie that did all the work. She walked in mother's shadow. She still does.'

'Oh, get off,' he said, hating the sight of her : the naked face with the eyes like an actress on the stage, the mouth spitting rubbish.

'And what about Rita?' She knew she was annoying him – the trick he had of twisting his head sharply as if someone had

82

fired an Ack-ack gun behind his ear – but she had to say it. 'She's just like Nellie, really. Keeping herself to herself, never saying anything important, just being proper.'

She hoped it was true : she couldn't bear to think of Rita getting into trouble – the shame of it, the gossip in the street.

'If our Rita is half the woman Nellie is, she's got nothing to be ashamed of.'

'But it's different times,' Margo cried. 'It's the war. People aren't the same. That sort of person isn't needed any more. The past is gone, Jack. Things are different now.'

'What sort of person?' he asked her, outraged, sensing mother and Nellie relegated to the scrap heap.

'People who had to be told what to do. There's things happening now that nobody can tell you what to do about. You can't act the same. That's why our Nellie gets so bad-tempered – she knows it's not the same.'

'Where would you have been without our Nellie?' he shouted, jumping to his feet.

The small blue indentures on either temple, marks of the forceps at his birth, darkened as blood suffused his face.

'God knows,' she cried, facing him in the unlovely room, 'but I mightn't have been all on me own.'

She trembled, filled with pity for herself and indignation that he thought so little of her. He was marching up and down the floor, twitching his head, struggling to contain his anger.

Margo was spent. She sat down at the table blinking her eyes to stop the tears from falling. She wanted to say : Your Rita, our Rita is going out with a foreigner, meeting him at this moment, going into shop doorways with him. She wanted to reproach him for stopping her belonging to Mr Aveyard, for the chances he had made her miss in the past. It was all his fault – his and Nellie's. All the rubbish he talked about wanting to go and live on a boat after the war, travel, see how the other half lived – his remembrance of poetry, his senti-mentality. It was all me eye and Peggy Martin. He was bound, like Nellie, hand and foot to the old way of life. It mattered to him what the neighbours said, if he caused gossip, if he owed money, if he seemed too much to be alive. He hated to have to look inside himself – the wicked women standing on Lime Street, the immorality, the heart beating raw and exposed like the pigs he slaughtered.

'I'm off,' he said. 'I'm not well. I don't need you blethering on, the way I feel.'

And he went. Tying his muffler about his neck in a paddy, squashing his worn Homburg hat on to his head.

'Why d'you think we're sitting here in the cold?' she shouted, following him up the hall, ashamed she was driving him away. 'All because Nellie won't have a fire in summer! I'm sick of it. Don't you blame me, Jack, if there's trouble.'

Out he went, slamming the door behind him, leaving her exhausted in the hall.

\*　　\*　　\*

Rita came back before Nellie – like a dog that had been whipped, her face asking for help.

'Oh dear,' said Margo, going through to put on the kettle. 'You silly little twerp, why didn't you tell me?'

'I want to die,' said Rita, dropping her coat to the floor and gazing about the room as if she was demented. He hadn't turned up at the station, he hadn't come to the bus stop, he hadn't said he would see her again. He walked away to the sound of the dance-band and she never saw him again.

'What happened?' asked Margo, wanting a full explanation before Nellie returned home full of talk about Valerie and her glowing secure future.

'He said I was a drowned rat.'

'Oh, he didn't!'

'He said: "Don't you ever wear nothing pretty, no dresses with frills?" '

'Oh, luv.'

'He said I was pretty as a picture, pretty as a rose garden.'

84

'Oh you are, little lamb, little pet, you are.'

'He never – he said I was a drowned rat.'

There was a storm of weeping, Margo crying with her, recalling other words from other men, time after time, years ago. They clung to each other, voices resonant with grief.

'When we were in the country, in the garden . . . he tried to – touch me. I pushed him away.'

'What did he do to you?'

'He tried to – well, he touched me – here.' She indicated with her hand the small swell of her breast. 'I pushed him away, Auntie.'

'Oh my God!' said Margo, rising to her feet, feeling old and responsible. She made tea and told Rita to wipe her eyes in case Nellie came back. Like something she had heard on the wireless, one of those educational talks late at night, she lectured her: 'Now look here, our Rita,' putting her heart into it, as if there was one more chance, the very last chance. 'You got to be decent, you got to have respect, but if you love him you have to give.'

In her mind a picture of George Bickerton undoing the buttons of his jacket, the drooping moustache painted on the boy's face, the unsure arms encircling her; the way his body trembled, the fear she felt, the stranger she was to her own flesh. She didn't know what to do, and neither did he. Never been talked to, never read any books, never known what it was to take off her clothes without turning away. A mist of ignorance, of guilty fumblings; it didn't matter about the church and that they were allowed to be in bed together. Nellie was in the next room, the blankets over her head. There was no excitement, no joy. It was the doctor tapping her chest, it was an illness.

'You mustn't lose him because you're feared,' she cried. 'You mustn't, Rita. I've read books since – it's natural, you shouldn't listen to Nellie. God knows, girl. Look at me – I'm a casualty.' She held her arms out dramatically as if she was on a cross.

And Rita did listen, she did appear to take notice: concentrating on her aunt, the black eyes shining like marble, the mouth grimacing with feeling, the thick body ensnared in the over-large cocktail dress.

\*     \*     \*

Rita wrote a letter to Ira in her lunch hour.

> Dear Ira,
>     I'm sorry if I annoyed you in any way but I do love you. I waited for you at the station for two hours, but you did not come. Please meet me next Saturday at 6.30 under the clock. I have got my Auntie Nellie to make me some pretty clothes so that you will be proud of me.
> Your loving Rita.

\*     \*     \*

She wanted to put kisses and even draw a heart, but it seemed common. After work she knocked at the Manders' front door and asked to see Valerie. Mrs Mander was curious to see her and eager to know about her young man.

'Lives in Washington, I believe,' she said, and Rita nodded, because she couldn't admit she didn't know where he lived, or how old he was, whether he had a mother and a father. 'He's got a dog and a goat and a horse,' she said, 'and a hen that sits by the fire.'

'In the city?' said Mrs Mander, taken aback.

Rita went into the front room with Valerie, bent her head shyly, twisted her hands about in their grubby white gloves, standing by the piano with the photograph of George, debonair in his sailor uniform.

'I want you to give a letter to Chuck,' she said.

'Oh yes,' said Valerie.

86

'Me and Ira had a quarrel.'

'I'm sorry about that.'

'Could you ask your Chuck to give him this letter?'

She took out the letter from her handbag.

'My Chuck doesn't know him very well, you know. I doubt if he sees him much in the camp. They're not buddies.'

It sounded like a tree about to bloom: Chuck and Ira on the same bough.

'I'd be ever so grateful,' Rita said.

She felt close to the older girl, dressed in such good taste, her plump left arm encircled in a bangle of shiny metal, her eyes sympathetic, not quite assured.

'Do you and Chuck have upsets?' she asked, trying to identify herself with them. 'Have you ever fallen out?'

'Everyone does,' Valerie said. 'Don't worry, luv.'

She was curious how Rita had ever gone out with the American in the first place. Rita was so put down, so without passion, living all her life with the old women down the road. As a child she had never played out in the street, never put her dolls to sleep on the step, never hung around the chip shop on Priory Road. In the air-raid shelter she wore a hat belonging to Auntie Nellie as if she was in church.

She stowed the letter away in the pocket of her jacket – not carelessly, with feeling.

\*　　　\*　　　\*

Rita was brighter than she had been for days. Setting the table for tea, humming as Aunt Nellie cooked the spam fritters on the stove. When Margo came in she couldn't wait to tell her what she had done, running into the hall when she heard the key turn in the lock, whispering in her ear that she had written a letter and given it to Valerie.

'That's good,' said Margo, tired from her day and wanting to sit down. Her moment of elation having passed with the night, she had spent the entire day brooding over the advice

87

she had given the girl. She wasn't sure of herself any more, she wanted to share the responsibility. She sat by the grate, and her handbag dropped to the floor and she let it lie.

'Sam, Sam,' said Rita, 'pick up thy musket,' and she and Nellie broke into little trills of laughter, the room filling with the smell of melting dripping.

*     *     *

Jack's shop was in Moss Street on the other side of the Park. When he saw Nellie, his eyes widened with concern at her having made the journey.

'You shouldn't have,' he scolded. 'Bogle told you to take it easy.'

'I wanted the exercise,' she said. 'I'm that busy on Rita's new clothes I had to force meself out of the house. I was straining me back.'

He sat her in the little cubicle at the back of the shop, perched on the stool behind the cash register, while he served his customers. He wore an apron, that Nellie made him, over his suit, with his coat sleeves rolled up. His small hands were always red and chapped from continually being doused under the cold tap in the back – he couldn't bear the contamination of the raw meat. He would have taken Nellie upstairs to rest, but he knew when his back was turned she would be washing his breakfast pots and tidying his bed.

'Was that Ethel Morrisey?' she called, when an old woman wearing carpet slippers had gone shufflling across the sawdust to the door.

'That's right.'

'By gum, she's aged.'

'We all have,' he said, dipping his head, in his Homburg hat, to avoid contact with the two rabbits hanging on a rail above the counter, bending over the marble slab industriously with a wet cloth in his hand.

Outside the window the errand boy balanced his bicycle

88

against the kerbstone and came in whistling. He had red hair and a great bulging forehead over which his cap wouldn't fit.'

'Hello, Tommy,' Nellie called, smiling and nodding at him through the glass of the cubicle. 'How's your mother keeping?'

'Me mam's fine,' he said, keeping his eyes down to his boots, hating to be noticed.

Jack told him to skin one of the rabbits, while he took Nellie upstairs and made her a cup of tea. He thought it would be nice to wrap one up for her and pop it in her shopping bag without her knowing. He had some difficulty bringing her down from the stool; she clutched at him as if she was drowning, leaving a pale dusting of talcum powder on the upper sleeve of his jacket.

She tried to shut her eyes to the state of the living room. She couldn't expect a man to keep it decent, and she supposed he did his best. It made her a little sad, the disarray, the neglect, as if he was homeless, about to move on; there were some things still in boxes and never unwrapped. And he never would move on, not now. It was a funny way to end up – he was a bigoted man in his views, and his surroundings were such a contradiction. He couldn't stand gipsies or Jews, or Catholics for that matter, and here he was in a pig-sty. In his person he was very particular, though : his ears, his nails, the round collars he took himself to be washed and starched at the Chinese laundry over the road.

'Whatever are you doing with that?' she asked, looking in bewilderment at the wind-up gramophone removed from its place behind the door and set in the centre of the hearth-rug.

'I was thinking maybe our Rita could use it. You know, when she's got friends in, now she's of an age.'

It was just an idea he had. He didn't think it would come to anything. He had never met any friends she might have had. Watching Nellie turning over the pile of heavy records, wrinkling her nose as he held one or two to the light to read the labels.

89

'They're a bit old,' he said, 'not very up to date.'

She was touched by his attempt to do something nice for Rita.

'Does it still go?' she wanted to know, wiping her hands together to free them of dust; and he told her it might, when he'd tinkered with it a bit – the spring seemed sound and that was the important part.

He made the tea and she sipped it, holding her cup with her little finger extended, as mother had taught her. She told him about Valerie Mander's imminent engagement, what Cyril Mander thought about it, when they were going to buy the ring, how they would have to celebrate. He nodded his head expressing interest, but she knew he detested Cyril Mander, and he didn't much care for Valerie or for Americans. He was narrow about people from foreign parts. He said they should have joined in the fight in 1939 and not waited so long. He said it was the Russians that were winning the war, not Uncle Sam. She often wondered what his attitude would be if he came face to face with a real live Russian, whether he would be so approving of them in the flesh.

'Chuck's a nice lad,' she said. 'You couldn't take offence at him.'

'It's as they say,' he said dourly. 'There's only three things wrong with them Yanks. They're overpaid, oversexed and over here.'

He got up saying he had to go downstairs to keep an eye on the shop, and left her to finish her tea. She looked at the mahogany cabinet and imagined what Marge would have to say about Jack's gesture and his choice of records: 'Just a Song at Twilight', 'Little Man You've Had a Busy Day'. She could just see the look in her eyes, the way her hands would fly up in a gesture of contempt. She put her cup down on the mantelpiece and peered at the photograph of Jack's wife with baby Rita in her arms – holding the infant wrapped in a shawl, as if she was scared she was going to drop it any moment.

Just then she heard the boy calling 'Eh Missus, come down quick!' And she trotted smartly enough down the uncarpeted stairs, holding her hand to her heart, seeing Jack as pale as death behind the chopping block.

'There's been a mishap,' he said, 'with the cleaver.'

'Where, you daft beggar?' she cried, fierce with shock. 'Where've you cut yourself, Jack?'

'Not me,' he said. 'Him,' looking at young Tommy who was standing at the foot of the stairs with his hands behind his back.

'It's nothing, Missus,' said Tommy. 'It were him that were took bad,' and he went to the back of the shop and put his hand under the tap.

Nellie made him run water over his finger till the cold almost froze him and the bleeding partially stopped. She struggled upstairs and found some sheeting to tear into a bandage. When she had wrapped his wound she told him to get off home and let his mam have a look at it. Already as he went out of the door the rag was darkening with blood. She felt irritated with Jack, slumped there behind the counter, perspiration beading his forehead – like a big soft girl, his face the colour of putty beneath his old black hat.

'Go and wet your face,' she said. 'It will bring you round.'

She couldn't think how he managed his business, feeling the way he did; slaughtering pigs, chopping up lambs, pulling the liver and the lungs out of animals.

The brown rabbit lay on its side, head partially severed, legs stretched out as if it still ran.

# 7

---

A LL Saturday morning Nellie stayed at her machine,
driving herself to finish one dress or another.

'I just want me black dress,' said Rita, looking in dismay
at the grey cloth with the stripe and the pink velvet alternately
running under the needle. Margo did the shopping again
because she knew how much Rita counted on a new dress for
the evening.

In the afternoon Nellie said she had a headache, and with
consternation Rita cried: 'Won't you finish me frock then,
Auntie Nellie?'

And Nellie said: 'Steady on, Murgatroyd, I'm only human.
What's the stampede?'

'I wanted me new frock for tonight. I'm meeting Cissie and
I want me new black frock.'

'Well, you can't get blood out of a stone,' said Nellie crossly.
'It's not ready.'

'But you said last night it was nearly finished.'

Nellie couldn't make out what was wrong with the girl,
standing there with her face all twisted up with desperation,
when only two weeks ago she wouldn't let them buy her a
new dress for love nor money.

'You wouldn't let me try it on you,' she said. 'You said
you had to wash your hair.'

Rita couldn't bear to be fitted. The touch of the dry tips
of her aunt's fingers, as they brushed the circle of her arm
or smoothed the material of the shoulder, filled her with

revulsion. She had to grit her teeth to stop from crying out her distaste. She had lived in constant intimacy with the elderly woman, soaped her white back in the rusty bath upstairs, nuzzled close to the flannel warmth of her at night. She couldn't understand this sudden aversion, when Aunt Nellie was being so kind, when she was working her fingers to the bone. At half-past four, when she knew it was quite hopeless, she ran upstairs and looked inside her wardrobe : the velvet, the blue satin, two years old, her day dresses, an old skirt – nothing pretty, nothing with frills.

'Oh please God,' she whispered, lying down on the narrow bed and burying her face in the pillow.

She thought with self-disgust of how she had refused a new frock from George Henry Lees, how she had nothing frivolous, no necklaces, no lace hankies, no shiny bangle for her arm. Marge came into her room and said that with a bit of adjustment they could do something with a brown silk dress in Nellie's wardrobe.

'It's old,' she said, 'but it's got a low neckline, it's very flattering.'

'I can't wear Auntie Nellie's dress,' cried Rita. 'I'll just have to make do with what I've got.'

But Margo brought the dress through on a hanger and asked her to try it on.

'Just try it, luv. Give it a chance.'

And it was smooth to the touch : it did make her feel silky and pampered, though it didn't fit.

'Look at the shoulders,' she said. 'Look at the waist.'

'Well, you'll have your coat on over it. I can pin it at the back.'

Marge combed her hair into a bun at the back like Valerie Mander sometimes wore. She took the stiff brown bow from the belt of the dress and pinned it with a kirby grip to cover the little tendrils of hair that wouldn't stay in place. She gathered the slack of the dress into a pleat and secured it with two safety pins. They hadn't any vaseline for her eyebrows, so Margo went downstairs and came back with a small smear of margarine on her little finger and it worked quite as well.

'What if he doesn't come?' said Rita, putting two small circles of lipstick on either cheek and rubbing it in with her finger.

'Oh, he'll come,' Margo reassured her, thinking it would be best in the long run if he didn't, best for Jack and Nellie. As soon as the girl was safely out of the house she was going to tell Nellie and rid herself of the awful weight of responsibility.

'Put some colour on your mouth, girl,' she said; 'you look like a corpse,' and could have bitten her tongue at the stricken expression on Rita's face : the child's forehead wrinkling up, the hair dragged severely back behind her ears, which were small and bloodless. Marge fetched the gold button ear-rings that Jack had given her last Christmas. She wished she could find the pearl necklace, but instead she brought a link of glass beads, orange and green, to clasp about Rita's throat.

'You look older,' she said. 'Look at yourself.'

Rita wanted to be glossy like Valerie, rich and glowing and warm. She saw her face with the dabs of pink on either cheek, the glint of gold at her ears, the green glass beads above the brown dress. In profile the beak of her nose was over-shadowed by her jutting lips, painted purple.

'I'm not pretty, am I?' she said in despair, and Margo said : 'Why, you look lovely, you really are a bonny girl.'

And Rita had to believe her, against her better judgment, because how otherwise could she survive, or go to meet him, or anything? She was dry and faded and slender in the brown dress, with her bold mouth pouting in distress. Being seventeen she couldn't imagine how much to be envied was the childish droop to her shoulders, the tender curve of her throat under the cheap glass beads, the gauche walk she achieved in Marge's best wedge-heeled shoes. It was only a quarter-past five and Jack had come in. She could hear him in the hall shouting to Nellie that someone or other had died. She was hungry,

94

unable to eat, lethargic, unable to sit still. Above all she longed to see Ira and feel that he loved her.

'I'll go,' she said to Margo, pulling on her newly washed white gloves and the macintosh with the flared back. She wanted to have time in the waiting-room at the station to smooth her hair and make sure her dress wasn't hanging down at the back. She said goodbye to Jack and Nellie, flustered by their comments – how smart she looked, quite the young lady. Knowing they weren't the right words, she wanted them to say she was pretty. She wouldn't take the two half-crowns Jack offered her. She said she had money of her own. She hadn't noticed before how old he was, how pinched his face was beneath the familiar hat, as he slid the money into his pocket. At the front door she was compelled to turn back and kiss her Auntie Nellie – the merest brush of her purple lips against the woman's powdered cheek. Even so, she left a mauve imprint to the right of Nellie's nose.

\*     \*     \*

She kissed Ira on the lips, standing on tiptoe and screwing her eyes up – out of gratitude and to show she wasn't prudish.

'You got my letter, then?' she said.

'Yeah,' he mumbled. 'That guy gave it to me.'

'Don't you know him, then? Isn't he a friend of yours?'

'I don't reckon I know him that well,' and he looked at her hair and away again and touched her throat with one finger and said, 'You didn't bury this one, then?' and she said 'No,' and was glad for once it was not raining or the wind blowing a gale up the dusty street. He said he wanted to take her to the movies : there was a film in Technicolour about a boy and a horse called 'My Friend Flicka'. She took his hand and after a moment withdrew her own and took off her glove, stuffing it into her pocket, so that she would feel the warm clasp of his fingers.

They had to queue up for the cinema on Lime Street, even

though they weren't going in the one-and-nines. She had never been treated to the pictures before by a boy, never gone in the back row among the courting couples. She was going to canoodle with him – she didn't care if it was common. But she dreaded lest the usherette came and shone a torch on them.

He was so tall, so neat in his clothes, the black tie tucked into his shirt just like Hitler, the crisp edge to his collar; she thought how well her brown frock toned with his uniform. All the same, it was agony to be with him, shuffling nearer and nearer to the entrance of the cinema, trying to make conversation, trying not to ask him why he had failed to come last Saturday. The way he looked at the drunk woman weaving across the road through the traffic, the insolent gaze of his eyes, the pressure of his hand on her shoulder. Every time he spoke to her, colour flooded her cheeks. She wondered how anyone survived being in love, let alone got married – condemned to live for ever in this state of quivering uncertainty. She had never been so aware of herself; she didn't know what to do with her hands, with her feet. There was grit in the corners of her eyes, in her nostrils, she could feel the lipstick caked at the corner of her mouth. How vunerable she felt, how miserable and happy by turns. The pain of being with him was almost as dreadful as living life without him.

\*    \*    \*

Seeing it was such a fine evening, Jack carried the kitchen chairs into the back yard for him and Nellie to sit on. Marge refused; she said it was mutton dressed as lamb to be sitting out there in all that concrete. They'd be asking next for a striped umbrella to sit under. She opened the kitchen window and sat at the table watching them, Nellie with her hands folded piously in her lap, Jack smoking his pipe full of tea-leaves. The tilt of the yard as it sloped down to the back alley gave them a precarious look. Any moment, she thought, they might slide slowly and uncomplaining into the brick wall. She could hear fragments of their conversation.

'. . . in a good way of doing.'

'At the masonic dinner . . . well thought of . . .'

Murmuring together in the evening air and a lone Spitfire, high in the washed-out space of sky, banking in a wide circle before heading out to sea.

'Ah well . . . comes to us all in the . . .'

'God rest his soul.'

Margo shouted through the open window: 'Did Rita say she was meeting Cissie Baines again?'

They both ignored her, placidly arranged in the back yard with little particles of soot floating down from next door's chimney. She thought of Rita meeting her young man. She thought of Mr Aveyard and her old job at the dairy where he was the manager – sneaking out to meet him when Nellie was busy at her dressmaking, making excuses on a Sunday afternoon for not going with her and little Rita to feed the ducks in the park: the time Nellie had given her daffodils to put on mother's grave and she gave them to Mr Aveyard instead. He hadn't known what to do with them, you could tell by his face. He held them upside down at the side of his trouser leg like a sunshade that was partially open. They'd pulled down the byre for the cows in Allsops Lane, and in a way it was a blessing. When they had made her give him up she'd had to leave her job at the dairy, and it was unsettling to hear the sound of the cows mooing in the early morning, waiting to be milked; it reminded her of him. He was getting tired of her long before Jack put the kybosh on things. He couldn't stand the way she had to slip out behind Nellie's back. He used to say, 'Why, you're a grown woman, Margo, what ails you?' and he was so set in his ways, so careful about money – no go in him at all. There was a certain coldness about him, a detachment in his wary brown eyes. Jack said anyone who had survived the trenches in France was bound to be touched – they'd been to hell and back again. In the

97

end she was grateful for Jack's interference, though she would never give him the satisfaction of knowing. When she had run to Mr Aveyard in tears, telling him Jack had said she had to give him up, he had stood like a statue in the little office behind the dairy, as if he didn't know that he should say 'Come to me, you stay by me, Margo.'

There was something very like alarm in his eyes. He never put his arms about her as she clung to him. 'I'm not going back home,' she cried. 'I'm never going back there.' 'It's a bit awkward, Marge,' he said. 'Our Nora's coming next week with the children. You can't stay with me.' So she sat on Lime Street station all night, telling the policeman she had missed her train to London, walking back to Bingley Road in the dawn, seeing Nellie asleep at the front window with Rita on her lap. Nellie said the child had fretted all night, but when Margo held her arms out to her she whimpered and hung back. She wouldn't go to her at all.

She looked out at Jack and Nellie in the yard, silent now, isolated in the little square of brick. Their complacency filled her with a kind of frenzy, the way they had of being content together, shielding each other from the outside world. Out there, over the network of decayed alleyways and the stubby houses, the city had turned into Babel, the clubs and halls filled with foreigners, the Free French and the Americans, the Dutch and the Poles, gliding cheek to cheek with Liverpool girls to the music of the dance bands, while Jack and Nellie sat through their Saturday evening talking about funerals. No wonder Rita had taken a leap in the dark.

She rose and went through to the scullery, standing on the back step, arms folded across her chest.

'Young Rita's courting,' she said. 'She's been meeting him for weeks.' And was rewarded by the turn of Nellie's head, her face shocked as if Margo had just broken something in the front room.

\*     \*     \*

She was watching the boy running through the yellow grasses – a thin boy, bleached by the sun, all the music swelling up, as he ran like a deer under the blue sky to the horse beneath the willow trees.

Ira kissed her. Kirby grips slid from her piled up hair. The boy slowed to a walk and held his hand out; the horse quivered against the green leaves, its coat chestnut-coloured in the sunlight.

The little brown bow slipped sideways from her hair and fell under the seat. He put his hand over her ear and all the sounds became confused, receding beyond his spread fingers, the boy's hoarse voice coaxing the animal, the music of the orchestra, the rustling of their clothes. Her neck ached with the effort of keeping her face turned to his.

When he let her go she touched her mouth curiously with the tips of her fingers. She felt her lips had swollen.

The mother of the boy stood on the verandah of the clapboard house, shielding her eyes from the sun. A dog ran among the scratching hens, and she flapped her apron angrily. The dog grovelled on its belly, its tail sweeping the dust. The hens squawked, dipping their beaks in search of the uncovered grains of corn. At the boundary fence a man in overalls was driving posts into the ground. He raised his sunburnt face and called to the woman : 'Ain't no sign of him yet?' and she shook her head. 'Don't you fret, woman,' he said. There was a close-up of her face, the back of her hand rubbing at her rosy cheek, her eyes on the land and the blue hills beyond the fields.

Ira gathered up the skirt of her dress; he was crumpling it into the palm of his hand like paper. She sat as if she was not aware of what he was doing. The whole cinema was filled with the noise of her rustling dress, drowning the music, the man's voice as he called to the dog.

Ira slid his hand across the top of her stocking and touched her leg. She shivered with apprehension and shame, knowing all the people in the cinema were watching her, waiting for the lady with her torch to catch the glint of her suspender.

There was a finger like a stick, poking at her, scratching her skin. She had to bite her lip to stop from pushing him away.

The blond boy was nuzzling his head against the belly of the horse, stroking its flanks slowly and reassuringly. He slid in his blue overalls over the neck of the animal, holding loosely the beautiful chestnut mane. Now the boy rode the horse towards the hills. Its tail streamed in the wind. The boy's bleached hair blew back from his face and he smiled in the sunshine.

'Stop it,' whispered Rita. 'Just you stop it.' And she gripped the skin of his wrist between finger and thumb and gave a vicious little pinch.

He withdrew his hand and they sat without moving for a long time.

On the screen the boy was crying, standing at a five-barred gate with his knuckles clenched, tears rolling down his cheeks, wood smoke in the air behind him, Mom in her long dress and little tendrils of hair curling about her face.

Ira reached for her hand, clamped in her lap with the nails dug into her palm. He uncurled her fingers one by one, held them loosely in his own.

She watched the boy move with dejected shoulders toward the house – dragging his boots in the dust, passing his mother without looking at her, head hung low.

In her lap she could see Ira's watch, luminous in the dark, feel his little finger move like a snail in the palm of her hand. Round and round. She thought of the girl at school who had told her what it meant, she knew what the signal for acceptance was, she had only to move her thumb back and forth across his. But she could not bring herself to do it. Maybe it meant something else in America, maybe she had misunderstood. She shivered. It was more disturbing to her, this minute sensation in her palm, than anything he had done before.

Face down on his cot the boy lay. His mother sat down on the patchwork counterpane and said : 'Don't fret, son. Reckon it's no use.'

Ira was shifting in his seat, fiddling at his belt to get comfortable. He was lifting her hand in his and guiding it down somewhere in the dark; she felt the edge of a button, a fold of cloth, something cool like putty, adhesive under her touch. She tore free her hand and sat with pounding heart, watching a blur of land with sun shimmering on a field of corn.

*　　*　　*

When she got home Uncle Jack was still there – sitting on the edge of the sofa with his hat and coat on as if he had been waiting. Auntie Nellie sat on her chair with her knees bunched together. Margo came to stand in the doorway of the scullery with her flannel in her hand and her eyes red as if she had been crying.

'I've told them,' she said. 'I had to, it was my duty.'

'It's alright,' said Rita, and she meant it. She thought it was outside her control. She stood there waiting, with her hair hanging down and her face composed.

'You've lost an earring,' Nellie said.

'I haven't. It's in me pocket.' She drew out the gold button and laid it on the mantelpiece alongside a reel of grey cotton.

'You shouldn't have been so underhand. You should have told us.'

She kept silent, rustling in her macintosh, looking at the remains of the tripe supper on the table, an inch of brown hem showing beneath her coat.

'Why you had to pick a Yank beats me,' said Jack. And Nellie interrupted fiercely : 'Be quiet, Jack. No need for a song and dance.'

He tossed his head like Flicka, dilating his nostrils as if he was a thoroughbred and offended into the bargain.

'We'll have to meet him,' Nellie said. 'You'll have to ask him here.'

Margo came out of the scullery, her face waxen from her wash. She went out into the hall without speaking and they could hear her footsteps going upstairs. The cat brushed against Rita's ankles. She bent and picked it up in her arms, rubbing her cheek against its fur.

'Don't do that, Rita. You don't know where its been.' But she took no notice.

'Sit down, chickie,' said Uncle Jack. 'We only want to do what's right,' and he patted the sofa for her to sit beside him.

She struggled past the table and sat next to him with Nigger on her knee.

'I believe his father has a business in Washington,' said Nellie. 'What would it be exactly?'

'I don't know,' she said, head down to the beautiful warmth of the cat.

'How old is he?'

She shrugged her shoulders and shut her ears to the questions. Jack said they'd brought her up decent, he was sure she was a good girl. He laid his hand briefly on her knee and patted it. She looked down at Margo's shoes. She thought she was a good girl, but she didn't know for how much longer. He hadn't talked about marriage. He had never said he loved her. The shoes were a size too small. Her toe hurt.

'Are you listening, Rita?'

'Yes, Auntie.'

Uncle Jack reached out his hand; the cat shifted its paw. He patted her knee again, trying to make contact. And she remembered. She had slipped on a piece of soap in Auntie Nellie's bathroom. When she was small. Taken her nail off under the door. Moaning in the big bed that her footie hurt. Auntie Nellie slept and Marge grumbled in her sleep. 'Be quiet, Rita. The sandman will get you.' She clambered out of the bed and stood on the cold lino, wandering up and down the landing, whimpering, screwing up her face in case the sandman should throw his dust in her eyes, until Jack, waking on the sofa in the room below, called: 'What's up? Who's that?' He bathed her foot and wrapped it in a hankie lumpy with Germolene, tucking her up on the sofa with him for comfort. She snuggled close to him and it was as if a spark had leapt from the fire and seared her skin – only it was something damp and cold, like a small animal, that plopped from the front of his combinations and touched her wrist. She recoiled in shock, lying wide-eyed in the dark, and he said, 'Is it still paining, chickie?' And she said it was, holding herself stiffly in case the thing lolling on the sheet should touch her again. She turned her head from the cat and watched his face as he talked to her, the eyes under the hooded lids, the beak of his nose overshadowed by the brim of his black hat, the even curve of his imitation teeth. He was attempting to explain, with Nellie's help, what troubled them.

'All that bothers your Aunt Nellie and me – I think I can speak for Auntie Nellie –'

'All that bothers us –'

'– you don't do anything you'll be sorry for.'

'I don't want you led into temptation.'

She could only stare at him. She tried to make her expression docile, she tried to appear receptive.

'We only want to do what's best for you. You ask him round to the house and we'll have a talk with him.'

'What about?' Rita asked.

'Don't play silly beggars,' Nellie said. 'We only want to be easy in our minds.'

'You must see that,' cried Jack. 'You do, don't you?'

'What's up with Auntie Margo?' said Rita.

'Just as long as he's decent,' Jack said.

He rose to his feet and said he must be away to his bed. He couldn't quite leave – there was something he hadn't made plain. It was as if he hoped miraculously the words he needed would come to him. The habit of speech was lost to him, he could only talk platitudes.

'Alright then, Nellie,' he said, awkwardly touching her shoulder; and she nodded her head at him, her face bleak.

'It never rains but it pours,' he told her, trying to make light of it, and she nodded again, her eyes mournful as if she had known bad weather all her life.

103

# 8

___

Uncle Jack came into the office at lunchtime to take her
out for a sandwich.

'But I've got my sandwiches,' she said, 'in my handbag.'

'Never mind. Give them to one of the other girls.'

She went into the cloakroom to get her coat, upset at his
arrival. Ira had promised to telephone her one day at work
and she dreaded leaving the building lest he should call while
she was gone. She didn't know any of the girls well enough
to offer them her sandwiches, so she left them on the ledge
under the wall mirror.

'Get in the lift,' said Jack; but she refused, preferring to
run down the five flights of stairs to the tiled entrance, watching the lift with its ornamental gates creaking and winding
down the well of the building.

'What's all this, then?' she asked, when they were walking
to a public house that he knew.

'I was in the town,' he said, 'on business. No harm is there?'

He wanted to get to know her better; he felt he had
neglected her in the past. With her new awareness, she
recognised the fact and resented him. He had left her alone
too much – he hadn't been a good father, or a good uncle.
He'd just stuck to the edges like the frieze on the wallpaper.

'I mustn't be late back,' she said, hearing the ring of the
telephone in her head. Every step they walked took her
further away from his voice.

'Get on,' he said. 'You've a good hour.'

They cut across the bomb site beside the Corn Exchange. There was a crowd of people watching a man lying down in the dust, with a lump of rock balanced on his bare chest. He was quite old. He had a piece of string tied about the waist of his trousers. On his arm was tattooed the figure of a woman with a red mouth. His partner was carrying round a trilby hat, shaking it, asking for pennies before he began his act.

'Go on, Uncle Jack,' said Rita. 'Give him some money.'

She was curious to see what the man intended to do. But Jack kept his hands out of his pockets.

'I thought you were in a hurry,' he said.

'I want to watch.'

Stubbornly she pressed forward to take a closer look. The man put down his trilby hat and went towards a mallet lying in the rubble.

'I intend,' he shouted, making a great show of spitting into his palms, 'to break that piece of rock before your very eyes.'

Grasping the handle of the mallet in his hands, he swung it in an arc above his head and brought it down. The man on the ground gave a low groan. He pointed his boots towards the sky and arched his back.

'It's a trick,' said Jack. 'It's all me eye and Peggy Martin.'

'Ssssh,' she said, watching the man's clenched fists as he lay in the dirt.

The man with the mallet gritted his teeth and swung again. Down came the mallet head. The man beneath the rock shuddered. The boulder split into three pieces. The mouth of the tattooed lady opened as the man's fist relaxed.

'Come on,' said Jack, not wanting the hat to be passed round again.

In shop doorways, in windows, Rita sought a glimpse of her reflection. She was constantly on the lookout for herself, to see if she was worthy of Ira. She had taken to wearing her hair brushed back to one side, showing an ear. It made her feel womanly to touch the fine strands of hair that freed themselves and swung across her cheek.

'You might have combed your hair,' Jack said. 'You look as if you've come out of Scotland Road.' She walked sullenly behind him into the Caernarvon Castle.

He kept looking about for people he might know, fellow butchers, men in the meat trade. He sat facing the doors with a look of expectancy in his eyes. It embarrassed her, the eagerness with which he watched each new arrival, the disappointment when he was not recognised. She drank her shandy and thought her nails were growing longer.

He asked her if she'd heard from her young man yet, and she quite bit his head off, snapping at him like Marge. He tried to be patient. He told her he'd noticed the way she looked at the necklace Marge was wearing the night of Valerie Mander's party.

'What necklace?'

'The pearl one your Auntie was wearing.'

'What of it?'

Disturbed by the truculent way the girl spoke to him, he managed to control his bad temper. God knows, he was only trying to be affectionate. She'd gone all sly, twisted inwards away from him, slouching there with her mouth sulky and her hair all over the place.

'I just noticed the way you looked at it. I've got one or two pieces of your mam's tucked away at home. I thought you might want them.'

She almost laughed, the way he put it. It sounded as if he'd cut her into squares and hidden her about the place. After all he was a butcher.

'What pieces?' she said.

'There's an engagement ring and a watch I gave her. A brooch – nothing valuable – but you're getting to an age.'

'I don't want them.'

He couldn't make her out. She had grown all flushed in the face, as if he had said something to annoy her.

'I only thought it would be nice for you,' he said.

'Leave me alone.' She was violent. 'You're always wanting

to do what's nice for me just lately – I didn't notice you bothered much before.'

He was stunned. She was a different girl. He had nourished a viper in his bosom.

A man in a black overcoat, a newspaper under his arm, came into the saloon. He stopped when he saw Jack, bent to take a closer look, and put his arm about his shoulder like a brother.

'Well, I never!' he said. 'It's Jack!'

'Walter!' cried Jack, jumping to his feet, his whole face illuminated in welcome. 'Walter Price!'

Rita thought it absurd the fuss he was making, the way he shook hands repeatedly, the way he murmured the man's name, over and over as if they were sweethearts. Walter had a little moustache that had turned grey at the edges. He kept darting glances at her, not sure who she was.

'It's Rita,' said Jack finally. 'You remember young Rita, surely.'

Walter didn't remember, Rita could tell, but he shook hands with her, unbuttoning his grubby leather gloves and holding her fingers tightly. Jack and he had an argument as to who should buy the first drink.

'Let me, Jack.'

'No, Walter, no, no, I insist.'

Off he went to the bar leaving Walter alone with Rita.

She wondered what she should do if Ira had telephoned while she was here. She didn't know where to phone him back. She didn't like to ask Valerie Mander – it would make her look as if she was doing all the running. Walter Price was telling her something, bending forward intently in his seat.

'Why, I remember. You're Nellie's girl!'

She looked at him coldly.

'I last saw you when you were a little lass no bigger than that,' and he held his hand out above the floor on a level with the table edge. She stared at the lino and the space between his spread fingers, gazing at an image of herself when small.

'Just a little slip of a thing —'

'I'm not Nellie's girl,' she said. 'I'm Jack's daughter.'

Walter had a lot to tell Jack about his business in Allerton. He'd expanded, done well for himself.

'Three vans!' said Jack. 'My word, you have done well!'

At the back of his mind he was hearing what Rita had said to him about the past. It hurt him, it stuck like a thorn in his flesh, the memory of her words. As soon as Walter went to the bar to buy his round, he said : 'I can't make you out, Rita.'

'What have I done now?'

'What you said before. I'm very hurt.' He drew in his mouth as if to stop his lips from trembling.

'Oh yes,' she said sarcastically. 'I'm sorry about that.'

'What do you know about anything?' he hissed, hating the look on her face. 'What do you know about my life ever since your mam passed on. D'you think I liked being on me own, giving up me house and me family?'

She gazed down at the floor, impressed by his show of emotion.

The presence of the girl inhibited Walter Price. And Jack was not himself. When he mentioned the old days in Allerton, he could swear the man's eyes filled with tears. The girl sat watching them, holding her head disdainfully. After a time the conversation died away. Rita excused herself and went into the lav beyond the bar. She leaned her head against the tiled wall and prayed he hadn't rung – rehearsed what she would say when he did : 'Hello, Ira! Yes luv, it's me – by the way, Auntie Nellie wants you to come to tea – she wants a little talk –'

She was filled with despair; she knew he wouldn't come. What would she tell them at home? It would make her seem despised, as if he wasn't serious about her. He won't come? Why ever not? Auntie Margo would give that laugh of hers, contemptuous, looking at her with pity. For all her chat about giving and the importance of not holding back, she would be the first to sneer, to lash out with her tongue : 'Couldn't you hold him then, Rita? Let him slip through your fingers, did you?' He was telephoning now, the bell was going in the outer office and Alice Wentworth, the one with the big chests, was answering it, talking to Ira, bold as brass, saying no Rita wasn't in, but would she do – making an arrangement to meet him, sitting in the pictures and not bothering to push his hand away. She started to cry, screwing up her eyes to make the tears flow. It eased her. She thought of Uncle Jack, all alone in the rooms above the butcher's shop, wearing his funeral tie, giving his little girl away. She thought of the picnic by the corn field, the way he bandaged her sore foot, the visit to the house in the woods. Before Ira, nothing hurt, nothing saddened to this extent. If there had been less space in her life before his coming, he would not have taken up so much room.

She powdered her nose and went back to the two men. They had been talking about her.

Walter said : 'I believe you're courting. An American, too.'

She blushed, though she liked what he implied. She smiled at him and he wondered what he had done to please. She shook hands with him, told him it had been nice meeting him. Jack went with her to the door. Across the street there was an old woman in a black shawl selling flowers. He wished he could buy Rita some carnations.

'I'm sorry I was nasty,' she said, looking away from him.

'That's alright, chickie.' But his voice was unsteady.

They stood for a time in silence. Jack cleared his throat and asked : 'Is your Aunt Marge behaving herself lately?'

'It's Auntie Nellie you want to watch. She's gone on a vinegar trip.'

His mouth opened in surprise. 'What's up, what's she done?'

'Auntie Margo says she's selling the furniture.'

'She's what?'

'There's things gone from the front room.'

'What things?'

'I don't know. Auntie Margo says a table's gone and a bit of china.'

'I don't believe it.'

He slapped his thigh hard and a woman turned to look. He couldn't credit it. Nellie would never part with mother's bits and pieces. Why, that front room was like the British Museum to Nellie.

'There's an explanation,' he said. 'She's having you on.'

She had to go, it was past her dinner break. He kissed the edge of her hair and she brushed her mouth against the collar of his coat and ran across the street away from him – passing the flower-seller all in black, with her shawl wound about her body, and the silver earrings dangling from the pierced lobes of her ears.

*        *        *

Margo knew him as soon as she saw him. It wasn't just fancy. She couldn't claim really to know men – she wasn't sophisticated like Valerie Mander. But as soon as she saw the boy's eyes, blue and incurious, she knew what sort of a man he was. For he was a man, for all his lanky limbs and the smooth cheeks that he obviously didn't shave. The way he entered the kitchen and saw them all standing there, devouring him with their eyes. It was as if he was on a hill-top, lazily watching a distant landscape. He was empty inside, he used no charm, he wasn't out to please; he passed his hand over the pale stubble of his hair and sat where he was placed. Nothing touched him : unlike Marge he had been washed clean of apology and subterfuge – he was wholly himself. At no time while he was among them, answering their questions in his flat laconic way, did she receive the impression that he was stirred by any chord of memory – no longing for mum or dad, for home and country, the things he had left behind. She looked down at the blue table-cloth – not Nellie's best, she hadn't gone overboard – at the plates from the sideboard in the front room, each covered with a small portion of tomatoes, lettuce and cucumber. The tomatoes Nellie had grown herself in a seed tray on the back wall – ripened them on the shelf in the hall, above the door. He took it all for granted, he would never be grateful. Suddenly she wanted to gather up the seed cake and the plums and milk and tell him to go away and never come back. Instead she listened to Jack, in his best suit talking about the other war and all the brave young men gone in France.

He didn't flicker a lid; he let his eye slide over Jack as if he was a reflection on the water. He ate his salad and his plums and spooned jam on to his bread. After a time his callousness excited her. She was wearing a plain brown skirt and a cream blouse – Nellie had told her not to overdo it. She leaned her elbow on the table, fingering the buttons at her throat. She wanted him to know that she saw through him, she wanted him to notice her. Jack said he must find it strange being in England after the bigness of America.

'Don't you find the British are insular, being an island race?'

And Margo said quickly: 'Whatever does insular mean, Jack?' because she knew Ira wasn't educated; she could tell by the set of his face that he was untouched by schooling. Nellie always said that the church was an education in itself – the rhetoric, the vocabulary it gave the ordinary working men and women, the hymns with their warlike phrases that expressed so much: 'Onward Christian Soldiers', 'Fight the Good Fight with All Thy Might'. You could tell by his conversation just how lacking in scripture he was, how ungodly – there was no ring to his speech, no cadence. She felt sorry for Rita, fiddling with the remains of her meal, crushed under the weight of her infatuation for him. She was disappointed for herself; it would have been nice if he had been like Chuck, warm and bouncing, bringing whisky into the house and manliness, making life rosy, every day like Christmas.

'Marge,' said Nellie sharply, 'help clear the salad dishes.'

In the scullery she was fierce with her. 'Pull yourself together! What's got into you?'

'He's no good,' Marge said, slapping the best plates into the bowl with gaiety.

'He's a nice enough lad.'

'Get off. He's no good.' And she rammed the tap of the cold water full on, drowning Nellie's protests. Margo felt as if she had been drinking, she found his company so unsettling. She was tired to death of them all being so polite to each other.

'Now Ira,' she said, when she had rinsed the plates and the bowls, 'I'm sure Nellie and Jack are anxious to know how you live in America.' And he smiled at her, slow and casual, lounging back on the settee with Rita huddled beside him, her face solemn with pride and ownership.

Nellie thought he was a nice boy: remote and shy perhaps, but that was better than him being brash as she had feared, flinging his weight about and playing the conqueror. Jack said they were invaders; they followed a long line beginning with the Vikings. Instead of the longboat they used the jeep: roaring about Liverpool as if they were the S.S. But Ira wasn't like that. It would be easy to steer Rita from him. He wasn't a threat to mother's furniture.

'I believe your dad has a business in Washington,' she said; and he said he reckoned he had. He wasn't a show off. He didn't elaborate. God knows how Marge knew, but she said his dad was in real estate.

'That's right, Mam, I guess he's in real estate.'

He helped himself to another round of bread. Jack had always maintained that they fed their army like pigs for the market, but he was wrong. Ira seemed starved of homely food, the sort his mother might put on the table.

'Have you any brothers and sisters, Ira?'

'Two brothers and four sisters.'

Up came Rita's head as if hearing it for the first time.

'Are you Catholics?' asked Jack, and Nellie waited with baited breath because she knew what Jack felt about Romans, but he said no, they weren't anything special, and Jack relaxed and sat back on his chair fumbling for his tobacco.

'My word,' said Margo, 'that's quite a family.'

She had a certain yellowish pallor that irritated Nellie, a melancholy look in her eyes that gave her the air of a tragedy queen. She was always putting herself in the limelight. The young man never took his eyes off her. He kept his hands away from Rita. He never put his arm round her. Nellie had been at the Manders earlier in the week and seen the way Chuck behaved with Valerie. Valerie knew how to take care of herself, of course, but it was dreadful the way he couldn't keep his hands off her – sitting on the sofa, imprisoning her in his arms, with everyone looking, and Mrs Mander smiling and looking through the pattern books as if it was something to shout about.

Jack wavered between hatred and pride – pride in his daughter that she had got herself a young man, and hatred of the blond stranger in his tell-tale uniform, a product of a race of mongrels, the blood of every nation in the world mingling in his veins – nothing aristocratic, nothing pure. It was astonishing he hadn't a touch of the Jew or the black in him. And that drawl of his – bastard English, with its lazy vowels and understatement. Jack didn't care for the way he looked at Marge – familiar, as if they came from the same back yard. He was probably only pretending not to be the least bit interested in Rita, to throw them off the scent. He hated to to think what he was like when he was alone with her. He wished Rita's mam could be here. She would know how to cope with it. He had a dim recollection of her determined sickly face, peppered with freckles, her sharp eyes that missed nothing, watching which way the wind blew.

Marge was telling one of her stories about her experiences in the factory.

'– you wouldn't believe what some of them get up to. In the explosives room behind the main building. It's a regular thing –'

They all watched her, drained by her vitality, the tea finished with, all the bread used up and the jam in its bowl.

Rita wanted to be down town with him, kissing in the pictures. He was so far away from her, sitting on the sofa next to her, listening to Aunt Margo. She had been surprised how easy it had been getting him to come home for tea. He hadn't telephoned – she lied, she said he had; she had fled to the station with her heart in her boots in case he should not be there under the clock. The trouble the family had gone to, the tins of food, the polishing of the front-door knocker, the pressing of clothes ready for his arrival. Fancy having all those brothers and sisters. She daydreamed they were married, going up soon to the little back bedroom together with everyone's blessing – no raised eyebrows, or telling them to be back before dark. They wouldn't go up to do anything dirty – just lie there under the eiderdown with Nigger stretched out across her feet. It wouldn't be like it was now. They'd be more like friends. They'd like each other. She hated the way he watched Margo. As if she was something special.

They played cards after tea. He didn't really get the hang of it; he said he'd never played rummy before.

'You just collect one of three and two of three and one of four and so on,' explained Rita.

But he held the cards in his hand as if he was blind. Jack thought it a point in his favour, he wasn't the gambling type.

'Let him keep the score,' said Nellie, fetching pencil and paper.

But he was loath to do it. In the end Jack ruled lines and wrote their names upon the paper in his beautiful copper plate.

Valerie Mander came at nine o'clock, holding her white arm out above the table, fluttering her fingers to show off her engagement ring.

'Oh, how lovely,' cried the aunts, catching her hand and taking a closer look at the small white stones. Rita didn't introduce her to Ira; she wished she hadn't called. She looked so beautiful standing there in a blue costume with her long red nails and her ring that proved Chuck cared for her.

Chuck was going to buy them a fridge.

'A what?' said Nellie.

'For food,' explained Valerie, 'to keep it fresh, like.'

'What food?' said Margo comically; and they all laughed, thinking of the meagre rations inside the coldness of the lovely new machine come all the way from America, sitting round the table, sharing her good fortune, as if it was normal to have a crowd in on a Saturday night – drinking tea, dropping cake crumbs on the carpet with a fine display of carelessness. The light began to fade from the room; the yellow drained out of the beige wallpaper. From next door's yard came the grieved sounds of pigeons calling.

Rita was restless and unhappy again. She took the milk jug and pretended it needed refilling, going away from the voices and the clattering cups into the scullery, leaning her head against the back door. She could hear Marge's voice, full of vivacity and nerve.

'When we were guarding the Cunard Building he said he could never get on with his wife. If you ask me –'

As she ended the story her voice rose in raucous vulgarity: a storm of hilarity, little trills of noise from the women, a man tittering strangely – not Uncle Jack – like a sheep running across a field. With shock she realised it was Ira. She had never heard him laugh before. It wasn't even a conversation, it was a monologue, the demanding tones of a giddy girl being the centre of attraction. And she wasn't a girl any more. Auntie Margo was an old woman with hollow cheeks and little veins that bled under her skin.

Uncle Jack came into the scullery looking for matches. He wore a delighted grin; he was good-humoured with the jokes and the company. He saw Rita against the door, her head on the stained roller towel, her face turned to him with the eyes wounded, like some animal at bay.

'Ah, chickie,' he said softly, 'come on, what's wrong?'

He was distressed by the sight of her. It was easy to comfort her; she was like a little child again.

'I'm not going back in there.'

'Don't be a silly girl. You don't want to be upset by your Auntie Marge.'

The urgency of the situation made him sensitive. He did see in a flash what ailed her.

He unbolted the back door and took her out into the yard, mellow with the last rays of the sun. They might have been in the country, the soft clouds in the sky, the cooing of the pigeons. He put his arm about her shoulder, leading her up and down the slope of the yard. He surprised himself, pacing the slate squares with the lupin plant wilting at the wash-house wall.

'You've got to take into account the fact that your Auntie Marge was a married woman. You're a big girl now, you're not a little lass – you know what I'm getting at –'

His fingers stroked her shoulders in the black dress with the white collar. 'The little maid,' Nellie had called her, but she did suit it. It gave a dignity, a simplicity that you couldn't help noticing. A little collar like a cobweb – cream lace, and cuffs to match. She was like something in a picture frame, an echo of the past. He was moved by her suffering, he wanted to pass on experience. He hadn't lived that long; he hadn't been through much, beyond death, his wife, and the hell of the trenches.

'What's she going on at Ira for?' wailed Rita, tired of his meanderings.

'She's not, our Rita,' he said. 'You don't understand.'

He could see Nellie peeping at them through the lace curtains, her face puzzled, not knowing what he was doing, walking Rita up and down the yard.

'He keeps looking at her.'

'He doesn't. Don't be daft. Listen, your Auntie Marge is a remarkable woman.' Till he said it, he didn't know it himself. 'She's not like Nellie and me; she's a different cross to bear. I can only surmise –'

It was a lovely word, he dwelt on it, turn about turn up the brick yard, till Rita said, 'What do you mean?' plaintive like those damn birds next door.

'When she was little, she wasn't like your Auntie Nellie and me. It was more difficult for her. She had a hell of a time. She never took what mother said for gospel. If mother told her to do anything she had to know why. Nellie and I used to think she was daft. She questioned everything. She made it difficult for herself. You're like her, pet.'

And again with the utterance, he felt it to be true.

'I'm not, I'm not,' she said, shouting the words like someone demented.

God knows what the people next door thought. They'd probably seen the American arrive and thought the very worst. Rita in the family way and he trying to make sense of it.

'You haven't done nothing with him, have you?' he asked, but she didn't seem to hear.

'Why am I like her?'

'Well, she wouldn't accept what was right and proper. I used to think she put it on, just to be awkward. But it's real enough. Nellie understands her, you know. You mustn't take any notice of their upsets. Marge has got more feeling than the rest of us.'

'What feelings?' she asked weakly, like a lamb left out in the snow.

'She always thinks the best is yet to come. It isn't. She never gives up.'

'She does.' Her voice was spiteful, but he continued:

'She doesn't mean to bewitch your Ira. It's just her way.' He stumbled over the phrase; he felt he was echoing what she already feared. Bewitched was such a bold word: it had overtones. 'When we were little she caught on quicker than the rest of us. I don't want to burden you, but I could tell you things about when we were little that would curl your hair.'

'What's up, Jack? What's going on?' Nellie was at the back step.

'Nothing, woman. We're just chatting.'

She went away unconvinced. He knew she would be upset, leaving their guests that way.

'What things?' Rita was puzzled by him. The weight of his arm across her shoulders bore her down.

'It was strict then. It was different those days. Spare the rod and spoil the child. I was beat on me bare flesh with a belt. Marge was beat regular. You don't realise. I didn't.'

He took in the window of the house alongside Nellie's, the fall of a curtain as somebody hid from view. All along the street, the curtains tight drawn across the windows although it wasn't yet dark – a row of boxes bursting with secrets.

'But your Auntie Marge would never learn. She wouldn't give in. She wanted to get married again, you know, when you were little.'

'She gave him up.'

He didn't think she had remembered. 'She didn't want to. We made her. It didn't suit your Auntie Nellie and me. She didn't want to be on her own with you. I didn't want her living with me. Not then. I'd grown used to it.'

'Used to what?'

'Being on me own. When your mam died and your Auntie Nellie took you in, I got used to it. After a bit. It wasn't my fault. I'd been chivvied by women all me life.'

'I want Ira to love me,' she said, as if she hadn't heard one word he'd uttered.

'It's not what it seems,' he said.

'I don't want him looking at Auntie Margo.'

'Talk sense.' It was ridiculous what he was trying to do. She wasn't of an age. She wouldn't understand love was mostly habit later on and escape at the beginning. He couldn't make a silk purse out of a sow's ear. 'Just wait here, our Rita.'

He had got out of his depth. Something in her stubborn face, her sad eyes, had shaken him outside the confines of his relationship with her. He couldn't continue. It wasn't for him to explain; only time could make it plain for her.

'Wait on,' he said, 'wait on, chickie.' He went forcefully into the kitchen, seeing Valerie Mander's white throat flung back in abandon, Nellie smiling like a clown, the young American with his eyes glued to Marge as if he was mesmerised. 'Ira, Rita wants a word with you.'

They went all quiet, but he had to go. He knew that much. He felt powerful when he was alone with the three women – superior, as if he had touched the heights.

'You don't want to encourage him,' started Nellie; and he said : 'Hush up, Nellie, I know what I'm at,' scratching the skin behind his suspenders that held up his green socks. A midge must have bitten him, though God knows it was unlikely, the rotten summer they'd had. It was the bloody cat. Flea-ridden thing.

*     *     *

'I thought you said you didn't talk much,' Ira said, 'you and your folks. Seems like they never stop talking.'

'It's my dad,' she said, 'he's gone balmy. I've never known him like that.'

'What he want to talk to you about? He was out here some time.'

He lounged against the wall of the alleyway, watching her push the back gate ajar with her foot.

'I didn't think you noticed.'

'I guess I better go,' he said. 'I got to catch the train.'

She didn't want him sleeping on the settee, not with Auntie Margo and Valerie in the house. It was all spoilt – there seemed nowhere they could be without her feeling miserable.

'It's a lovely ring, isn't it?' she said, seeing the little white diamonds pale above the curved red nails.

'How old are you?' he asked, staring at her in the gloom.

'Seventeen. How old are you?'

'Older.'

'Not much.'

Someone was tapping on the window. She let the yard gate swing back and block them from view.

'Will you telephone me at work?'

'Sure I will.'

'You didn't last week. I waited. If you don't, shall I just come to the station?'

'I guess not. I may have no furlough. I don't have every Saturday.'

He'd turned his back on her. He was pulling at a weed growing in the cracks of the wall.

'But when will I see you?' Her voice was breaking in despair.

'I'll call you. I'll do that. But I guess I won't make next Saturday.'

'Couldn't we go to the country again? I could take time off work. We could go to that place again.'

She was begging and she knew it. She was saying she would go to the empty house on the shore and lie down with him. She might have a baby. It was practically sure she would, but she'd take the risk; she'd do anything as long as he would see her.

'I guess I don't have no furlough next week.'

'Rita, Rita.' It was Nellie calling from the back door. She didn't want them like a couple of cats yowling in the back alley.

Rita had a melancholy feeling she would never see him again, never love him, never be given the chance to show how much she cared. All her life she had been waiting for him, beyond the house in the woods with the stuffed hen in the window. He was the people in her dream that caused her so much fear. He was the loved one who could come to harm. When she screamed in the night it was for him; when she saw the naked statue in the flower-bed it was an image of him wrestling with an angel. He had to love her. Give her time, she would prove to him how much she had to share, beyond the dirtiness, the scrabbling at the elastic of her knickers. She would die for him if he would let her.

'I'll call,' he said. 'Reckon I'll telephone tomorrow.'

He left the house before Valerie Mander, not kissing Rita, sprinting down the road to the Cabbage Hall to catch his tram to the station.

# 9

A T WORK Margo put her name down on the list for the
Dramatics Society. They wanted extra people for the
Christmas Pantomime. Ever since she was a child, people had
told her she should go on the stage. There was no end to the
facilities in the factory for recreation : football and snooker
for the men and keep-fit for the ladies; lectures in the dinner
break on how to make the food more interesting, how to make
old stockings into novelties for birthdays. She hadn't partici-
pated before, but with the winter coming and the approach
of the festive season it would be nice to be with a lively bunch
of people, larking about and rehearsing songs. She wouldn't
tell Nellie right away, not until she was accepted; there had
been words between them over the way she had behaved to
Rita's young man. She protested indignantly : she said she
wasn't going to sit in silence all evening, not with everyone
else acting as if the cat had got their tongue. It would be a
relief to get out of the house one evening a week. Maybe it
was that summer was ending, the thought of the winter to
be endured, that made the house seem charged with emotion
and tension : Nellie carting bits of furniture up the stairs –
she'd caught her red-handed with the bamboo stand – Rita
going about the house heavy-eyed and dreamy, alternately
singing to herself as she prepared for bed, and sitting on the
sofa with a face like death, unable to speak, not troubling to
turn the pages of her library book. Now and then Margo
caught a glimpse of such vulnerability on her sallow features,

such despair, that she was forced to look away. She would not interfere. Rita must come to her. It was almost a week since Ira had been to tea. Once he had gone from the house Margo forgot how threatening she had found him, how unsuitable. She remembered only that he was very young with not much to say for himself. Nellie had been over to visit Jack in the week. Jack said he was afraid Rita was going to get hurt – she was obsessed by her Ira. Nellie seemed to have other things to occupy her mind. She refused to explain why she was storing things in the box-room. Since her turn in the car she had quietened considerably, the sting drawn from her character. She did her housework with an abstracted air as if she was planning something. Between the two of them, Margo felt the house to be depressing. Once or twice she went down the road to the Manders'. Prompt on seven o'clock the jeep came bouncing up the road. Valerie would run to the step. It made Margo laugh the way Chuck leapt from his vehicle almost before the engine had died, propelled into her waiting arms as if he was catapulted across the pavement – flowers in his arms, crushed against her blouse, roses, carnations, little feathery sprays of fern; burying her face in them, her cheeks glowing like the bouquet he had brought her; the two of them always laughing and cuddling, calling each other honey and baby, like on the pictures. He was always bringing them presents – he was a regular Santa Claus : packets of cigarettes, a gold lighter for Valerie, a wrist-watch for the absent George; always whisky on the sideboard, tins of food in the pantry, packets of real butter in the new fridge. Margo could see Jack's point of view – it was a bit like the invasion troops looting the land and the Manders fraternising with the enemy. No wonder the rest of the neighbours looked askance at the jeep swinging up to the door. The contrast between life at Valerie's and the gloom that pervaded Nellie's house was almost too much for Margo to bear. It was as if she ran to shelter from a great black cloud that was gathering in the sky.

On Saturday night Rita didn't get ready to go out. She

lay upstairs in her room and told Margo she had a headache.

'But won't Ira be waiting for you?'

'No, he wont. He's training this weekend.'

'Training?' said Margo.

But Rita closed her eyes and wouldn't say another word. All week she had waited for the telephone to ring, though she knew it was useless. She was wallowing in self-pity and withdrawal. She had no friends, no hobbies, no interest beyond Ira. She hated him for being so cruel to her. She dreamed of revenge, of someone in the office telling him, when he did at last ring, that she had left to get married : one of those sudden romances, Alice Wentworth would tell him, a naval officer, a Dutchman. She recalled the seaman billeted on them in the first year of the war, his homely vacant face, the civilian suit he wore, dull and shabby, the little black suitcase he carried with his uniform inside. Auntie Margo had liked him. He bought her some material for a dress once. He took her to look at his ship, though she said she wasn't allowed on board. She saw Ira in his mustard jacket, his black tie; under the jaunty angle of his cap he lowered golden eyelashes to cover eyes that were the colour of the sky. She lay moaning on her bed, wanting to hit at him with her fists.

'She can't go on like this,' said Margo to Nellie, 'lying up there fretting. She's not eaten a thing all day.'

'Give her time,' replied Nellie. 'She'll come round.'

'They've not had a tiff,' Margo said. 'He's just training. There's no call for her to act like this.'

Nellie was cutting out the body of Valerie Mander's engagement dress. The noise the scissors made, as they sheered through the material and scraped the surface of the table, irritated Margo.

'How much did that material cost you?' she asked.

'Four shillings a yard,' said Nellie.

'You were done. I saw some just like that in Wharton's window. I swear it was a bob cheaper.'

'What Wharton's?' asked Nellie, not looking up.

'That shop near Ethel Freeman's house. Round the corner from where Frisby Dyke's used to be.'

'Ethel Freeman never lived near Frisby Dyke's,' said Nellie. 'You're thinking of someone else.'

'Get away. I went there regular.'

'Not Ethel Freeman,' Nellie said again.

It made Margo mad the way Nellie never gave up, never admitted she could be wrong. She was like a bull terrier with its teeth dug in. She would die rather than let go.

'I've joined the Dramatics,' she said, daring Nellie to make a scathing remark.

But Nellie didn't say it was foolish or wonder how long that little phase would last. 'That's nice,' was all she said, bunched up against the sofa as she snipped at the curve of the arm-hole, the tip of her tongue caught between her teeth with the effort of cutting straight. She wanted to make a lovely job of the dress. She was very fond of Valerie. For all the differ-ence in their attitude to life she could admire the girl. Never underhand, Valerie gave the impression she knew how to deal with living. She was confident. Nellie had thought of giving her the dress as a present, but no one had ever mentioned a wedding or given any indication of how long the engagement might be. They were going to have a party – everyone in the road invited, people from the camp, relatives from Yorkshire, a really big do. No one knew how much longer the war might last, whether Chuck would be sent abroad. It was all indefinite.

'If the war ends,' said Margo, 'will Chuck stay on, or will Valerie rush off to America?'

'How do I know?' Nellie said, 'you see more of them than I do.'

Jack came and they listened to Gilly Potter on the wireless talking about Hogs Norton. Rita stayed upstairs. Jack called her down for a cup of tea and a cream cracker, and she wan-dered round the kitchen like a stray animal, scattering crumbs from her mouth, slopping tea into her saucer.

'Get away!' cried Nellie, fearing damage to the green taffeta on the table. So she ran upstairs again, tears of affront in her eyes, slamming her bedroom door in a temper.

\* \* \*

On Tuesday Margo was told to come to the Dramatics room the following evening for an audition.

'A what?' she cried appalled. 'I can't do no audition.'

'We only want to hear your voice, girl. We're not asking for bleeding Shakespeare.'

On Wednesday morning when the alarm went for six o'clock she shut her eyes again, tight.

'Get up Margé!' said Nellie, kicking her on the ankle. 'Alarm's gone.'

'I feel terrible,' she moaned. 'I feel that poorly. I think I'll go in later when I feel more myself.'

'Get off, there was nothing wrong with you last night.'

But should couldn't very well drag her out of bed, she couldn't dress her and push her out of the door. Marge stayed where she was till mid-day, waiting till Nellie went out shopping on Breck Road.

'I may pop over and see Jack,' Nellie called, listening to Marge wheezing in the bedroom. Marge didn't reply. She was lying upstairs, right as rain, smoking her cigarettes in bed.

Margo wanted to be really ready for the audition. She washed all over and shook some of Nellie's talcum powder inside her corsets. She was bound to get sweaty, being nervous. She tried singing the chorus of 'I Do Like to Be Beside the Seaside', but she broke into a fit of coughing when the band played 'tum, didly um tum tum'. She put her earrings on, and a bracelet, and pinned a brooch to the front of her dress. Then she unpinned it, because she didn't want to seem to be trying too hard. It was her talent they were after, not the crown jewels. When she was going downstairs, someone knocked at the front door. She saw the outline of a man's

126

head outside the glass. It was Ira. She led him through into the front room. Afterwards she didn't know why. No one ever went into the front room unless the vicar called at Christmas, or in case of extreme illness, like when George Bickerton died. It was typical of him, she thought, that he didn't look at the room, didn't notice the furniture from another age : the good carpet on the floor, the photographs sepia-coloured with eyes black as coal, Mother grimly smiling.

'Whatever brings you here?' she asked. He handed her a packet of cigarettes. She was taken aback : he didn't smoke himself.

'I rang Rita at work,' he told her. 'She said you were sick.'

'I'm not. I've got a –' She stopped because she didn't want to admit anything. He was looking at her opening the packet of cigarettes.

'Just a chill,' she told him. 'I'm off out now to me work. Did you want to see Rita?'

She knew he didn't. He knew damn well Rita was at work. She was scandalised, and yet there was a little bubble of excitement in her, getting bigger and bigger at the thought.

'Now look,' she said, 'let's get one or two things straight.'

But when she looked at his face, she wasn't sure she was right. He looked so innocent, so without guile, boyish with his bony face pale, twisting his cap in his hands. She lit a cigarette. It was no use giving him the packet back – not these days when they were so scarce.

'What have you come for? You know young Rita's at work.'

'I wanted a word with you, Mam, you being more a woman of the world.'

The audacity of the boy! What did she know of the world, cooped up in Bingley Road like a ferret down a hole?

'I reckon I can tell you. I ain't going to see Rita again.'

She didn't know where to flick her ash. Nellie had taken the bamboo stand up to the box-room.

'I can't see her no more.'

'Well, you best tell her yourself. You've no cause to be telling me.'

'I thought you could break it to her. I tried to tell her, but she don't seem to listen. I don't aim to harm no one.'

'Why can't you see her?'

Inside it was doing her the world of good. She hated herself for the joy she got from his words. He didn't want Rita; Rita wasn't going to find the happiness that she herself had missed. She caught Mother's eye, that stern and selfish orb. She stared back boldly. Mother couldn't use the strap any more, not where she was.

'I guess she's too young, Mam. And she's kind of joyless. She don't want no fun, no drinking nor dancing.'

'But she does,' Margo protested. 'It's just she's unsure of herself. We haven't exactly taught her to enjoy herself, her Aunt Nellie and me. I mean I've tried, but it's Nellie that's the power behind the throne.'

She felt ridiculous, telling a complete stranger the intimate details of their life.

'Rita sure sets a store by what you say. You could tell her. I mean, you've known grief, Mam.'

'Grief?'

'Your husband dying. You know about men. The kind of books you read.'

She looked at him, not fully understanding.

'What books?'

'Rita told me about the sort of books you read. She found one in your drawer. You know about men. You could square it for me.'

She couldn't credit Rita had got hold of that book. She'd searched the house from end to end, day after day, trying to find it. She thought she had lost it at work. She went red with shame thinking of Rita reading that filth, Rita reading those dirty words.

'I've got to go,' she said. 'You'll have to excues me. I must be off to my work.'

He stood up, never taking his eyes from hers. He was a bad one, she knew for sure: the cocky way he looked at her, the little tinge of colour in his no-good face. She was devastated by the uselessness of her personality. The kind of men who fancied her – George Bickerton, Mr Aveyard, the chap on the tandem, the Dutch seaman in the box-room. They were attracted to her at first. And it was precisely the glitter that drew them at the start that drove them away in the end. They couldn't stand her at the end. She wished she was Bette Davis, Joan Crawford, languidly sitting in a long dress, calling them darling, sipping her cocktail, loyal and loving always – but cool like a snake, telling them to go before they told her. She threw her cigarette into the hearth, on the virgin tiles that Nellie scrubbed each day though never a fire lit the grate. She walked briskly into the hall and said it had been nice talking to him, but he better go now, she would be late.

'I'll call again, Mam,' he said, very polite, not smiling; and she shut the door after him and put her hand to her heart to catch her breath.

She was so agitated on the tram, in the audition, over Ira and his boldness, that she hardly noticed her voice singing, 'We'll meet again. Don't know where, don't know when'. She clasped her hands together, opened her throat and sang. They accepted her at once; they said she would be an asset. She felt very little satisfaction.

*　　*　　*

Nellie was furious at Marge going out like that. Thinking her safely in bed, she hadn't bothered to take a key. She had to wait for half an hour on the step until Rita came home from work.

'God knows what came over your Auntie Marge,' she said. 'I left her ill in bed. Wait till I see her.'

Rita was so happy she peeled potatoes and made Nellie a cup of coffee.

129

'Sit down,' she said. 'I'll get the tea.'

All her face was light and curved. Gone the morose set to her mouth, the desperate look in her eyes.

'Ira rang,' she said, unable to keep it to herself. 'He's busy training. He can't see me this week, but he rang me up to see how I was. He's been chosen for some course – they're sending him to Halifax for three days. He's going to write me a letter.'

She was a different girl; it was amazing the effect a man had on a woman. Nellie had seen it before in Marge, the fluctuations of mood, as if the man held the reins and drove as he pleased. It left her cold. She had been too busy nursing mother to experience that sort of thing – blacking the grate, preparing the food, seeing the boys went off to work decent. Time had gone like the pages of a book flipping over.

\* \* \*

When Marge came in she never said she was sorry for gadding off like that. She wasn't contrite about being late home.

'Auntie Nellie was locked out,' said Rita. 'She had to wait on the step.'

'I wasn't to know you didn't have your key,' cried Marge, belligerently.

She tried to get Nellie off to bed early so that she could talk to Rita. But Nellie wouldn't budge – taking her stays off and sitting by the empty grate for an age, yawning, stirring her tea. In the end Margo went up first – she was that worn out – falling asleep without a thought in her head.

\* \* \*

The following night Nellie went to the Manders to give Valerie a fitting. As soon as she was out of the door, Margo asked Rita what Ira had said to her on the telephone.

'How d'you know he phoned?' asked Rita. 'I never told you.'

'I know, he did, that's why.'

130

'He's been chosen for some course. I'll probably see him on Saturday."

'He's not been chosen for any course,' said Margo. She couldn't put it tactfully – it wasn't the way – it had to be done like a bull in a china shop. She watched Rita's face, like smooth glass, not a line on it.

'He called here yesterday.'

'He what?'

The glass splintered. Furrows appeared on her high forehead, her mouth puckered in surprise.

'He called. He called to ask me to –'

It wasn't that simple. She felt like Jack, slashing the throat of a young pig, letting its life's blood soak into the sawdust.

After a time Rita said : 'Asked you to what?' Her voice was hard like a stone.

'He feels you're too young. He minds about you.'

'Too young?'

'He doesn't want to commit himself.'

'What did he come here for when he knew I was out?'

'He wants to do what's best.'

'I told him you were off work.'

'He's a nice lad.' She felt like Judas, giving the signal for young Rita to be cut down by swords.

'He's going to ring me tomorrow – he said so.'

Margo didn't have the strength. The malice drained out of her. It wasn't competition – it was little Rita, without a mother and father. She wasn't even angry any more about the dirty book gone from her drawer. Jack and Nellie had moulded Rita, cramped her development, as surely as if they had copied the Chinese, binding the feet of infants to keep them small.

'He's been picked for a course,' said Rita stubbornly. 'He's going to write me a letter.'

\*        \*        \*

On Friday, Rita went straight from work to Uncle Jack –

surprised him in his braces, the shop shuttered, cooking his tea.
'Does your Auntie Nellie know you're here?'
'I just thought I'd come.'
He was cooking kidneys in a white pouch of fat, boiling a whole cabbage in the pan. She was hungry. She sliced the dark brown meat, rare with blood, and shovelled it into her mouth. She told him Marge had said Ira had visited her. She sprinkled pepper on to the cabbage and wiped her bread across the plate. The way she ate disgusted him. He had to put down his knife and fork and turn his head away.
'Who called on Marge?' he said.
'Ira. She said Ira called.'
'He never called to see her,' said Jack. 'It's Marge's way. She's trying to protect you.'
'What from?'
She was looking at him with her mouth filmed with fat.
'Just from getting upset. What's he supposed to have called for?'
'He said he wanted to do what's best.'
'There you are. What did I tell you? It's just Marge's way.'
He walked round the gramophone, still in the centre of the room, and went into the small kitchen, the paper peeling from the walls.
'Don't you mind the mess, Uncle Jack?' Rita asked.
He didn't like her criticising him – it wasn't respectful.
'I don't really see it. It's only temporary, this place. One day I'll buy meself a little boat and retire to the waterways. When the war's over.'
When the war was over, she thought, Ira would go home. Back to his big family and his father in real estate.
'What do you do when you work in real estate?' she asked.
'I'll tell you this,' Jack said. 'You're Ira's dad is never in business. He's a farming lad – you can tell. He's been raised near the soil – it's in his face.'
'He's been sent on a course. He's been chosen.'
Jack was relieved they weren't going to have a scene about

132

Marge. Whatever the truth of it was, the child didn't seem too upset.

'Do you think he did come round? I said Auntie Marge was off sick when he rang me in the morning.'

'I'm blessed if I know. Don't ask me, ask her.' He made tea and Rita put cups on to the table. 'It's always the same, when you get infatuated. It's like a virus in the blood. A perpetual state of fever. One time, I went on holiday and nearly died of love.'

'With me mam?'

'No, before your mother. I went on holiday to the Isle of Man and we played tennis on the back lawn. And there was this woman there that drove me out of me mind. I've got a photograph somewhere.' And he rummaged through the packing cases on the floor, looking for the image he remembered, finding himself in white trousers sprawled before a net with a young woman with a bandeau round her head and a smirk on her face.

'I loved her,' he said. 'I didn't think I'd survive. But I did. Went back home, caught the number twelve tram and met your mam on the top deck.'

'But why did you leave her on the Isle of Man?'

'She preferred someone else. Went off with him the last week of the holiday.'

He took the photograph from her and stuffed it away among the pictures of Nellie and Marge and Rita as a baby.

'You best be off,' he said. 'I don't want Nellie upset. She's a wonderful woman.'

He was always so anxious about Nellie, afraid she might have another attack. He gave her a piece of meat to take home.

'Passion,' he said, as he let her out of the shop, 'is a strange thing. Why I could have killed the fellow that young woman went off with. I'd have swung for him.'

*        *        *

133

Rita went down town on Saturday and Ira wasn't there. She came home slowly, dragging her feet along the road, not staying up for a cup of tea, going straight to her room with the pencil and paper she had ready in her handbag. Laboriously she wrote the letter:

Auntie Margo said you came to the house last week. I don't know if you did or not. She said you wanted to do what's best. What's best is that you should see me. You have not written me a letter as you promised. You have not telephoned me. Mr Betts sent me for stamps at the post office on Friday and I didn't like to ask if you had rung. Did you ring me Friday? I keep asking if anyone has telephoned me and it makes me feel foolish. They all look at me in the office. I went to the station tonight to look for you but you weren't there. Are you on your course? I saw all the other women waiting and I thought we were not like them. If you truly don't want to see me, please tell me. Please dear Ira, on my mother's head, please tell me. Your loving Rita.

When she read it again she crossed out the bit about her mother's head. It seemed out of place. She would go tomorrow to Valerie Mander and ask her to give Chuck the letter. It didn't matter any more if Valerie thought she was chasing him. She couldn't live another day waiting for that telephone to ring. She was worn out with waiting for the postman to come, worn out with tossing and turning in her bed trying to work out if Margo was telling the truth or not.

\* \* \*

Rita waited till Monday to give Valerie the letter – in case he telephoned Monday morning. Again she stood in the front room holding her white envelope.

'I know it's a nuisance,' she apologised, 'but I'm desperate, Valerie.'

134

She stared deliberately at the older girl, her lip quivering. She needed to enlist sympathy.

'But what's up now?' asked Valerie, puzzled. 'Your Auntie Nellie said he rang last week.'

'Yes, but he's gone to Halifax on a course and he said he'd write, but he hasn't. And he said he would probably see me on Saturday, but he didn't come.'

'On a course?' said Valerie. 'What sort of a course?'

'In Halifax. He's been chosen.'

'They don't go on courses. He's maintenance. He looks after the boilers and the electricity.'

Rita was insistent. There was a stubborn set to her jaw; she was polite but firm.

'I know it's a lot to ask, but Chuck did give him the other letter.'

'Well, he didn't mind the one about meeting him at the pictures.'

Valerie saw the look on the girl's face. Outside in the hall Mrs Mander was greeting someone from up the road, taking them up the hall, opening the kitchen door. The sound of the wireless was turned lower.

'I didn't want to tell you,' said Valerie, 'but Chuck told me about what was in the letter. He couldn't help it. He had to read it to Ira.'

'What d'you mean?'

Valerie was twisting the engagement ring round and round on her finger, feeling the three white diamonds in their setting of gold.

'Didn't you know?' she said. 'He can't read or write.'

It was too dreadful to take in. It was unbelievable, like Auntie Margo saying he had called at the house. She fled from the Manders', the letter crushed in her fist. She ran up the alleyway behind the houses. Once there had been meadows and trees, cows grazing, ducks on a pond – before they claimed the earth and built the wretched little houses : the industrial revolution, Uncle Jack called it, when they took the green and pleasant land and made it into a rubbish dump, with dwellings fit for pigs, the sky black with smoke from the factories, the houses built back to-back to conserve room – more bricks to the acre : a time when not many went to school, when education was for the few, when only the privileged could read or write. Her mind spun excuses for him : he had been ill as a child, he had been born in a desert far from the city. She saw him lying on a couch like the death of Chatterton with his arms spread wide; she saw him hoeing the sandy earth with a trowel, not a tree in sight. It was like learning he was blind or a cripple or a criminal. She didn't know how to cope with it. He was a dunce, her Ira, thick as a plank, not able to play cards, to read a book; he would never write her a letter. And at this thought hope surged up in her heart, she could have cried aloud with the enormous sense of relief. That was why he hadn't written as he promised ! He couldn't. He had gone to visit Auntie Marge to tell her he wasn't good enough for her. He knew Rita was clever at English, at composition. Nellie had boasted of the fact. He had come to Margo to say he was not worthy. Dear God, she thought, running up the cobbled alleyway, if he was that unschooled, he would need her, he would want to hold her in his life. She kicked the back gate open wide and strode up the sloping yard, not frightened any more.

*     *     *

Margo was disillusioned with the Dramatics Society. The cast seemed to be mainly workers from the crippled section. Apart from the principal boy and Cinderella, they all had one leg shorter than the other, or withered arms. The Ugly Sisters, two fellows from the explosives department, wouldn't need any make-up. They hadn't offered her a part. She was just one of the chorus. She sat around for hours after work waiting for the pianist to come, wrapped in her fur coat at the back of the hall. They wanted her to come on Thursday as well. Some big mouth had said Margo's sister was a dress-maker and they wanted Margo to give them some idea about costumes.

'It's Nellie that knows about clothes,' she said. 'I don't think I can come.'

But they insisted – they said she must pull her weight. She thought gloomily of staying late one night a week all through the winter, standing in the freezing cold to catch her bus home, her dinner lying shrivelled in the oven.

*　　*　　*

The feeling of hope inside Rita didn't last very long. He never telephoned. At work she put her fingers in her ears to deaden the sound of the bell that never stopped ringing. Mr Betts spoke to her quite sharply – he said she was slacking, she wanted to pull her socks up.

On the Saturday, hope died entirely. He wasn't under the clock. She waited for hours. She didn't want to go back home.

Nellie had almost finished the beautiful engagement dress; she was sewing the buttonholes by hand. Valerie said she felt the right shoulder was a wee bit out of line. Nellie unpicked the arm-hole and reset it. She wouldn't have taken notice of anyone else, but Valerie had an eye for such things. They were going to have the engagement party next weekend. Cyril Mander was decorating the front room; Mrs Mander had chosen new curtains. George might even be able to get leave. When Rita asked Valerie if Chuck had seen Ira, the older girl hated to tell her there was no sign of the boy.

'Chuck did look.'

'But where is he?' cried Rita.

'It's a big camp, you know, love. It doesn't mean he isn't there.'

Valerie didn't know what to say for the best. Chuck had made a few inquiries – discovered what section he was in – but the boy couldn't be found. Chuck said dozens of the young ones deserted every month – ran off to London with women. He certainly hadn't gone on a course – never to Halifax. She wondered if the girl was confiding in her auntie. Valerie felt responsible – after all Rita had met the young soldier at their house. She disliked the look of despair on Rita's face, the panic. It soured her own happiness. The girl was acting as if she was heart-broken. She hoped she hadn't got herself into trouble. It was just the daft sort of thing that would happen to someone like Rita – damp behind the ears, wrapped up in tissue-paper all her life, never exposed to the wind.

# 10

---

NELLIE was tired, but satisfied. She had worked full out on the lovely Valerie's dress. In the afternoon she pressed the skirt and draped the frock over the model. She went down on her hands and knees, crawling round and round the floor to make sure the hem was absolutely even. She had plenty of time. Marge wouldn't be home for a meal – she had gone to her dramatics – and Rita wouldn't want much, not with the poor appetite she had lately. They could have something cold, and she could go round to Valerie's after tea for the final fitting. There was a button not quite in line. She re-sewed it there and then, a little on tip-toe to reach, her eyes screwed up against the light. She sat down to rest and stared critically at the dress. The beauty was in the yards of material in the skirt, the low cut of the bodice. Mrs Mander wanted sequins but Valerie said no, it had to be plain. She saw Valerie whirling round and round like a film star, all her petticoats showing, her plump knees silky in her nylon stockings. She should ask Valerie to get Rita a pair of those nylons. It might cheer her up. It hadn't lasted very long, the courting of the young American. She hadn't needed to show her disapproval – he had simply vanished into thin air. Jack had said something about him calling one afternoon and Marge sitting in the front room with him, but he'd got the wrong end of the stick. Marge would be at her work and she would never dare take him into the front room, not without Nellie's permission. She stood and went through to see that everything was alright;

twitched the lace curtains into line, ran a finger along the mantelshelf. Funny how she didn't miss the rosewood table, the bamboo stand. It was as if they had never been. When Jack was in a good mood she would mention she wanted the sideboard shifting and see what he said. Marge said there were mice in the box-room; she wouldn't be surprised if they ate right through mother's furniture. It was on account of the pigeons they kept next door; there was always vermin. Marge only said it to upset her. She'd told Jack she was selling the furniture. If Jack hadn't known her better he might have believed her; he might have thought she was getting mercenary in her old age. It could have hurt him, after all the money he poured into the house – the bath upstairs, the decorating – and the money he gave each week for Rita. When they had been little, it had been Marge that had been the generous one. Jack was tight, but Marge would give you the shirt off her back. Life did funny things to people, manipulated them. But if you kept faith with God it was alright. She had prayed about Rita and He had listened. She wasn't thinking only of herself, she did know he was not for Rita – the way he held his knife and fork, the way he lounged all over the furniture. Chuck wasn't like that. He called Cyril Mander 'Sir'. He took his hat off when he entered the house.

Valerie popped in on her way home. Her gloves were real leather. She had a little fur tippet about her neck.

'Oh, it's lovely, Auntie Nellie, it really is.'

She stood in wonder in front of the green taffeta dress, touching the material of the shoulder gently with her fingers.

'The shoulder's alright now,' said Nellie anxiously.

'Oh, it's lovely! I didn't want to crush the skirt.'

'I'll come over after tea for the final fitting.'

'Come whenever you like,' said Valerie. 'I'm not seeing Chuck this evening. Our George is home on leave.'

She confided in Nellie that George didn't take to Chuck. Cyril said he was being bloody-minded. Chuck was being very understanding, giving the boy time to get adjusted.

George said the Yanks had taken their time coming into the war. Cyril said it was Roosevelt's fault, not Chuck's.

'George is jealous of his money,' said Valerie. 'He's jealous of his jeep – all the time off he gets. He hates Yanks.'

'Well, it's understandable, I suppose,' said Nellie; and Valerie gave her an old-fashioned look. When Rita came in a few moments later Valerie asked her if she would like to see her new shoes.

'They're green,' she said, 'with red soles. They're lovely.'

'I might come along later,' said Rita. She was listless; she had shadows under her eyes as if she hadn't slept. She curled up on the sofa and turned her eyes away from the engagement dress.

'Valerie looks a picture in that dress,' said Nellie, 'a proper picture.'

'I bet she does,' Rita said. But she didn't care if her aunt preferred Valerie to her. She had filled her mind during the week with so many variations, ways of finding him, reconciliations, scenes of the future, that now she was empty. There were no pictures left in her head – just a voice very small and demanding, crying for him to come back.

'You'd suit green,' said Nellie, laying the table for tea.

Rita saw no sense in it – green, blue, it was all one.

Outside it was raining again, the cat cried at the window to come in. All day he had sat in the meagre branches of a sycamore tree at No. 11 waiting for the ginger female to come out into the yard.

Rita wouldn't go to the Manders with Nellie; she said she would come round later.

'You'll be all on your own Rita,' protested Nellie. 'Your auntie won't be home for hours.'

When she had gone, Rita went upstairs into the front bed-room. She opened the drawers of the dressing table and looked inside Margo's old handbag. There was a nail file and an empty carton of cigarettes; a letter from a firm saying her application had been received. She dragged the black suitcase from under the bed : a dress rolled up in mothballs, an empty envelope with a Dutch postmark, Margo's gas mask, a little pen-knife made of ivory, a flat wallet with a birthday card in it and a ten-shilling note. She took the pen-knife and the money. She didn't need it – Nellie wouldn't take any of her wages – but she felt Margo owed her the ten-shilling note. There was nothing personal she could pry into, nothing exciting like the book she had once found. She went downstairs to fetch her coat.

\*     \*     \*

Margo was ready for Nellie to be scathing about her coming home early – the remarks about her having no staying power. She was going to say the rehearsal had been cancelled. It had in a way : in her mind at any rate, she had just stopped being interested – sitting about for hour after hour waiting to sing one song. When she let herself into the house she was grateful that no one was in. It was awful sitting with young Rita, watching her waste away for love of Ira. She saw the cat pressed against the window, waiting to be let in. She opened the back door wide and put down a saucer of milk. Outside it was close, the rain coming down softly, spotting the red tiles of the yard. She sat down to rest, spreading her legs to ease them. Reaching out to pull the evening paper from the sideboard, she felt something cool to her touch. It was George Bickerton's pen-knife. She couldn't think what it was doing under the newspaper. She held it in her hand and remembered him peeling an apple for her, long ago on a Sunday afternoon in Newsham Park. It had made her laugh the precise way he loosened the green skin, round and round till it dangled to his lap, exposing the white fruit, the blade of his knife glistening with juice. She went through into the scullery to boil a kettle. She stood at the open door, watching the rain. She heard footsteps coming up the alleyway.

142

Mrs Mander thought the dress was a perfect fit – for her taste, a trifle plain, but Valerie looked beautiful. Even George was enthusiastic.

'By gum, it looks good,' he said, 'even if it's wasted on a Yank.'

He was putting Brylcreem on his hair, making himself smart to go down to the pub with his father. Cyril thought the world of him – his sailor boy in his bell-bottom trousers, the white bit at his chest showing off his pink skin, the little jaunty hat on the hall-stand.

Valerie stood at the mirror, holding her skirts away from the generous fire, looking at the curve of her shoulders, the plump arms rounded beneath the green straps. She had a tilted nose, brown eyes with full lids, a mouth that perpetually smiled above a slightly weak chin.

'I'm not sure about the waist,' she said. 'What d'you think?'

'What's wrong with the waist?' asked Mrs Mander. She studied her from every angle.

'A belt, you mean,' said Nellie. Valerie was gripping her waist with her two hands, emphasising the fullness of her hips.

'I'm off,' said Cyril. He kissed his wife full on the lips. He was a man that never did anything without gusto.

'What d'you think, Nellie? D'you think a belt would round it off?'

Nellie thought she might be right.

'I could wear me brooch,' said Valerie. 'The one Chuck gave me.'

'Is Rita's young man coming to the party?' asked Mrs Mander. 'He's very welcome.'

Valerie and Nellie avoided looking at one another. When her mother went to put a hot water bottle in George's bed, Valerie said, 'How is Rita, Auntie Nellie? I'm that worried about her.'

But Nellie wasn't forthcoming, she had her pride. She wouldn't discuss young Rita in front of the neighbours. She said she thought Valerie was right about a belt. It would give the finishing touch. She had a piece of material at home that would do.

'Have a cup of tea first,' said Mrs Mander; and Valerie said gaily, 'No mum. Get out the whisky. Give Auntie Nellie a real drink. It'll put hairs on her chest.'

It was a vulgar thing to say, but Nellie took it from her. There wasn't anything Valerie could do to offend, in her opinion. Rita came in but she wouldn't take her coat off.

'I don't think I'll stop,' she said. She was shrunken in her white macintosh, a reproach to the happy Valerie. God forgive you, her face said; here I am, seventeen years old, without hope. She made the little room depressing, refusing to relax or sit by the fire.

'Have a drink,' said Valerie. 'Auntie Nellie won't mind.'

Auntie Nellie, who thought she minded, nodded her head in acceptance, seeing Valerie was in charge. There was something elderly about Rita, despite her youth. As if she was tired, aged beyond her years by her emotion : her eyebrows frozen in an arch like a comedian, the cupid bow of her mouth drooping like a clown.

'Haven't you heard yet?' whispered Valerie, when Nellie was in the kitchen helping Mrs Mander with the tea.

'No,' the girl said coldly, as if it was Valerie's fault. She stood by the yellow sideboard accusingly, her arms held stiffly, taking her drop of whisky in little sips as if it was medicine.

'Sit down, do,' said Nellie, irritated by the sight of her wilting by the door.

'I'm going for a walk,' she said, and off she went up the hall.

'Having trouble?' asked Mrs Mander, genuinely wanting to help. She could have said a lot years ago, when Rita was a little lass; she could have guided Nellie; but she was never consulted. You had to be careful with girls. They were like blotting paper. Boys were devils – they strode away without a backward glance. Girls were different. They lingered, kick-

144

ing against the pricks, stamped by the mother's authority. When they rebelled in earnest you had to look backwards to find the cause. She herself had only to look at Marge, her looney ways, her mode of dress, that business with the manager of the dairy some years before.

'She's shook up,' admitted Nellie. 'It will blow over.'

Mrs Mander hadn't any business to interfere. She looked at the lovely Valerie in her engagement dress and held her tongue.

\*　　\*　　\*

Nellie went home to cut out the belt. She said she would come back when it was finished.

'Rita,' she called up the stairs, hoping she had gone to her bed. She didn't like her wandering about Anfield late at night. Rita had made a show of her, acting so theatrically, not talking to Mrs Mander, never saying 'Thank you very much' for her drink. She thought that Valerie was right about the belt. She cut the material and sat down at her sewing machine, running the piece of cloth under the needle; snapped the thread with her false teeth; took up her scissors and snipped the loose ends free; turned the hem of the taffeta and leaned back in her upright chair to ease her back. She got such pains in her shoulders.

She took her foot off the treadle. She thought she heard something upstairs. The cat was crawling round and round on the newspapers behind the door.

'Give over, Nigger,' she said, turning to the machine.

There was definitely a noise upstairs. She clutched her hands in her lap and stared at the ceiling. She remembered what Marge had said about mice. Something scratched the floor boards, above the door into the hall. Something rustled. It couldn't be mice. The pigeon coops were on the ground floor, outside the scullery door. Mice couldn't be eating mother's furniture. They ate paper and cloth, not wood –

145

like the man in Germany who stowed a fortune away under the bed – bank notes – and found it shredded.

'Nigger,' she said, the scissors still in her hand, 'come on!' picking the cat up awkwardly in her arms, going up the stairs to the box-room. The cat hung over her arm, struggling to be free.

'Give over,' she murmured, anchoring it by the ears, puffing as she climbed.

She opened the door with the cat half over her shoulder, ready to flee down the stairs. It wasn't quite dark. There was a glimmer of light on the landing. Inside the box-room she saw first the bamboo stand; behind it the edge of the truckle bed, and two legs, white in the half light, the knees bunched together, a welter of stockings about the ankles, the feet turned inwards. He was standing up, buttoning his trousers, dressed, apart from his jacket, which was laid across the rosewood table – she could see the metal buttons gleaming. She backed away and stood on the landing. He caught hold of his coat and dragged it along the table. She heard the buttons scratching across the wood – a minute sound like a mouse scampering for safety. She leaned against the wall and the cat leapt from her arms and flowed down the stairs. He came out on to the landing with his jacket over his shoulder. Sheepish. He looked in the dim light as if he was ashamed of himself. He passed her, going to the head of the stairs with his head sunk on his chest. How dare he scratch Mother's furniture? A lifetime of sacrifice, of detailed care. What right had he to drag his clothing across the polished wood? She thought it was safe up here, away from the light of the window, untouchable. He was no good, he was disgusting. She could feel the anger gathering in her breast, the whole house was loud with the beating of her outraged heart. She raised her arm and stabbed him with the scissors – there below the stubble of his hair, at the side of his neck. She was that annoyed. He turned and looked at her, clutching the side of his throat, a quick decisive slap of his hand as if an insect had stung him. He was surprised. He

146

opened his mouth and his foot faltered on the step of the stairs. He flung out his arms to balance himself and he fell sideways, rolling down the turkey carpet, crumpling into a heap, his coat flying to the foot of the front door, and something like a spray of water cascading from his pocket, leaping and bouncing across the lino like sweeties burst from a bag. He bashed his head on the iron curve of the umbrella stand. Flung out a leg and knocked the little wax man from his pedestal. Hurled it from its glass dome. Sent it sliding and snapped in half among the imitation pearls. Opened his mouth in agony. Died before the air left his lungs.

The cat, crouching beneath the stairs, came out and sniffed at the floor. Putting out a paw it slapped a bead playfully and ran to the door like a kitten. Nellie came down the stairs slowly, sat on the bottom step and leaned forward to examine Ira. With her left hand she undid her fingers from the handle of the scissors, and put them away in the pocket of her apron. He lay with his face turned to the hall carpet. She had punctured the skin of his neck. There was blood oozing gently from the wound, staining the cream collar of his shirt. She went into the kitchen and shut him out in the hall, taking the scissors from her pocket and laying them on the table. She felt she had done wrong, but there were mitigating circumstances. He shouldn't have touched the furniture : he had no right to be in the box-room with her – her stockings round about her ankles and her white knees exposed. He had come into their lives and caused nothing but trouble – upsetting Rita, making a liar out of her. She thought of Rita as a little girl, riding a donkey at Blackpool, jogging up and down as she rode across the sand, running in and out of the waves with Jack's handkerchief wound around her head to keep the sun off, kicking her feet in the water. It would be better if children stayed small, never grew up, never knew how deep the sea could be.

'What are we going to do?' said Marge.

She stood in the doorway with her eyes wide open as if she

147

was standing in a terrible draught. Nellie couldn't look her in the eye. Not yet. The shock had been too great. The sort of things Marge got up to were beyond her. She couldn't have known what she was about. Even though she had been a married woman, she couldn't have understood what she was doing.

'I can't think,' she said. 'I can't get me thoughts.'

'We ought to tell someone,' said Margo.

'Wait on,' Nellie said.

She went out into the hall and looked at Ira again. He was very long and skinny. He lay with his leg buckled up under his buttocks. He hadn't moved.

Marge was looking at her, her hand twisting about at the waist of her dress.

'I've got to do Valerie's belt,' said Nellie. 'I said I would go back.'

'We ought to tell someone,' said Margo again, like a gramophone record – like Jack's records in the upstairs room above the shop, covered with dust.

'If we do,' Nellie said, 'there'll be talk. I don't want there to be talk.'

'But it's wicked,' Margo said, unable to keep her eyes from the man on the floor, with the little pearls scattered about his head.

'We haven't had much of a life,' cried Nellie. 'We haven't done much in the way of proving we're alive. I don't see why we should pay for him.' She thought 'wicked' was a funny word coming from Marge, considering what she'd been doing. She thought of them both being taken into custody and Mother's furniture left with the dust accumulating.

'Think of the scandal,' Nellie said. 'Whatever would Rita do? I only did what was best. He had no right to touch Mother's table.'

They sat on either side of the fireplace listening to the clock ticking. In the hall Nigger rolled beads across the lino.

'Whatever was he doing with that necklace?' asked Nellie.

148

But Margo was moaning, rocking herself back and forwards on her chair as if to ease some private grief.

After a time Nellie stood up and went into the hall. She pulled down the curtain from under the stairs.

'We best wrap him up,' she said.

'What for?' Margo asked.

'We don't want young Rita tripping over him.'

She was very capable, a dressmaker to her bones. She put the chenille curtain under the clamp of the sewing machine and made a bag for Ira. She made Marge drag him by the feet into the kitchen. He pulled the carpet sideways and his head bumped on the lino. At the side of his throat the wound looked as if he had been kissed by a vampire. There was a little bubble of blood about the edges. Nellie said they had to put him inside the curtain.

'What for?' said Margo. She was gormless, all the sense knocked out of her.

'We've got to get Jack,' said Nellie. 'He best come round with the van. We have to cover him up. You know how squeamish Jack is.'

They slid him into the bag. It was like turning a mattress; Nellie made Marge hold Ira in her arms by the sewing machine so that she could sew the bag up over his head. It had to be a proper shroud. Jack mustn't see any part of him. There was no cause to lay pennies on his eyes or cross his hands on his breast. He wasn't one of the family.

'Wait on,' said Margo.

She went into the hall bravely and gathered up the pearls, brought them into the kitchen and slipped them into the curtain with Ira.

'Whatever was he doing with that necklace?' said Nellie once more.

'I don't know,' Margo said, lifting him in her arms again and letting Nellie complete her job. 'He said Rita buried them in the garden and he dug them up when she wasn't looking. He thought I might want them.'

149

'What garden?' asked Nellie, snapping the thread with her hands, unable to use the scissors. Marge couldn't tell her.

'There wasn't time,' she explained.

She clasped him closer in her arms, felt the curve of his head against her breast, the length of his legs buried in the chenille curtain.

She ran up the road to the Manders' and said Nellie wasn't feeling too good. She wanted to use the phone to contact Jack.

'Shall I go up?' asked Mrs Mander.

But Margo told her not to bother. Nellie wouldn't want a fuss.

'You're to come at once,' she said to Jack. She knew the Manders could hear every word.

'Is Nellie bad?' cried Jack, alarmed. He shouted down the phone as if she was deaf.

'Just bring the van,' said Margo. 'Quick as you can.'

The heels of her shoes as she walked back to the house clicked like knitting needles. It was as if someone was following her.

They dragged Ira through into the wash-house in case Rita should come back. The cat thought it was a game, digging its paws into the material of the curtain, jumping skittishly into the air. Margo got the giggles when they had difficulty getting him through the door. She had to let go of him and lean against the sink.

'Give over,' said Nellie.

She was as white as a sheet, strong as steel. She never paused to gather breath. She pulled Ira down the back step into the dark and told Margo to open the wash-house door. She was used to carrying the dummy about. The screw had gone from the stand – you had to watch the body didn't fall away from the pole. She handled the curtain with skill. When they lumped him on to the concrete they snapped the head of the lupin plant. All its petals blew away down the yard.

When Nellie had manoeuvred him into the wash-house she still thought of things to do.

'Straighten the hall,' she bade Marge. 'There's a stair-rod broken. Throw it into the back.'

When Jack knocked at the door, she ran up the hall after Marge and told her not to let him in.

'Tell him to go round the back,' she hissed. 'Tell him to take the van up the alleyway.'

Jack cursed Marge – he thought she was playing silly beggars. He hadn't a collar to his shirt, just a stud. He looked like the vicar.

'Whatever's going on,' he said, coming in through the back door with his face all peaky with bewilderment.

'Sit down,' said Nellie. She told him very little beyond the fact that she had knocked the young American down the stairs. She didn't say what he was doing upstairs. Or why she had stabbed him with the scissors. Something had happened, she hinted, and she'd only done what was best. She knew by his face that he didn't want to ask any questions. He was too frightened. He didn't want to know.

'It was that umbrella stand,' she said, fingering the tape measure that hung about her neck. 'You always said it was a death trap.'

'Oh my God,' said Jack. He clutched the mantelpiece for support. 'Where is he?' he asked, after a moment.

'In the wash-house,' said Margo.

'Oh my God,' he said.

'We'll have to get him in the van,' Nellie told him. 'You'll have to take him down to the docks.'

'Oh my God.'

'You'll have to tip him in the river. That's best.'

'Oh my God,' he moaned again.

He couldn't help them. The two women had to take Ira from the wash-house and slither him down the yard to the van. They could hear Jack retching in the scullery.

'Take him,' said Nellie, when they were done. 'Take him

down to Bootle, Jack.' She held his face in her two hands, shaking him a little to give him courage. 'You're a good boy,' she said.

'Oh my God,' he whispered, going down the yard with his black hat jammed on his head. They waved to him from the back step.

When the gate shut behind him he felt very alone. He knew Nellie couldn't come with him on account of her health. But he hated being in the van with Ira in the back.

Nellie held her hand to her heart. The rain was pattering on the wash-house roof. She stood there for all the world as if she was taking the air.

\*       \*       \*

Afterwards she went through into the little front room, the tape measure still dangling about her neck, and allowed herself a glass of port. And in the dark she wiped at the surface of the polished sideboard with the edge of her flowered pinny in case the bottle had left a ring . . .